Following retirement from a industry, John Umfreville cho the family history and filling i The main success came with the linking of the English and Canadian branches of the family through exploration of the life of Edward, an employee of the Hudson Bay Company, which led to a reunion of the present day family branches at Sioux Lookout.

Separate research was carried out into the history of the malting trade at Henley-on-Thames and also into the politics and life of the most successful mayors of that town around 1900. This work unearthed a plenitude of unproven facts, stories, and gossip concerning life in this riverside town. This has been used to create a fictional story of a new Methodist minister and his family from India as they try to become accepted into the society of the townspeople.

Find out more at www.johnumfreville.co.uk

Best Regards

John Umfreville

The Comings and Goings of

THE

REVEREND

BERTRAM

MOOREHOUSE

John Umfreville

SilverWood

Published in 2019 by SilverWood Books

SilverWood Books Ltd
14 Small Street, Bristol, BS1 1DE, United Kingdom
www.silverwoodbooks.co.uk

ISBN 978-1-78132-837-8 (paperback)
ISBN 978-1-78132-850-7 (ebook)

British Library Cataloguing in Publication Data
A CIP catalogue record for this book is available
from the British Library

Page design and typesetting by SilverWood Books
Printed on responsibly sourced paper

This work is dedicated to Peter and Mabel,
residents of Henley who gave me Meryl – Jan

THE RIVER

For several thousand years the rain that fell on the chalk hills was collected by small streams which merged together, giving an increased flow to the water whose new power cut through the surrounding soil and stones to give a deep, fast flowing current. This stream now took the path dictated by gravity as it wound towards the sea. This timeless flow dictated the growth of nature's bounty during its floods and droughts which, in turn, influenced what species should thrive or fail. Humans adapted to the gift of water and communities grew up in response to their rich surroundings. Inhabitants living on sheltered banks, gathering crops and tending their herds, found the river difficult to cross and so they needed to manufacture crude boats of logs or reeds in order to reach the opposite side or the next village downstream. These boats also facilitated the catching of fish that lived in deeper waters and eventually gave the opportunity to trade with the big city founded by the Romans downriver. The river always offered a way of life for the gatherings of families who lived by its banks which enabled them to survive. Sometimes life was pleasant and sometimes the river enabled the inhabitants in the area to become prosperous.

The people of one such small settlement found a higher meadow on which to build their homes out of the reach of the annual floods but with only a short distance to cross to the pastures on the other side. This crossing point became widely known for its convenience since it gave travellers making their way from Winchester to Oxford on church business a shorter distance of fifteen miles to cover. These folks were pleased to pay a piece of silver for the convenience of the shorter journey given by the use of the villagers' boat and often they knelt on the far bank to give thanks for the blessing of time saved. It did not take long for the inhabitants to persuade the men who had already constructed the bridge in a town lower down the river to show how the river could be better crossed by a wooden bridge instead of a boat. Now travellers with horses and bigger loads could cross the river; grateful to those with skills who were the bridge builders. Those now living by the bridge insisted that a small chapel be placed in the middle to better encourage travellers to show their thanks with a donation to the Virgin Mary, to whom the bridge was dedicated. Later, when the original timbers started to fail, it was decided to rebuild it from stone – but not before a church had been built on the town bank. Thus the little church of St. Mary was erected. A small inn with a livery yard appeared over from the church and then various shops and trade stalls sprang up along the road leading from the bridge.

With the passing of time many changes took place throughout the country, bringing their pressures political, military, and church on the small community on the river bank. But the original geographical reasons for the convenient river crossing remained the focus of the town that grew around the road leading from the bridge. Farms at the edge of the town became estates whose inhabitants needed services to provide their comforts, and so more tradesmen arrived; vintners, shoemakers, haberdashers, butchers, and bakers. Foremost amongst all of these newcomers were the maltsters who were able to double the value of their barley by its conversion to beer for the townspeople, and to malt which they were able to send by river to London. These maltsters became the prominent citizens and a charter was purchased which gave the town the right to hold markets and to elect a council with a mayor. As the town became more important they agreed to pave the road from the bridge up to a market place, which was completed by the building of a market hall. Later a wall was built around the town to protect the inhabitants from the turbulent events of the times.

At this point the diocese of Winchester redrew all of the boundaries of the parishes under its jurisdiction. The small stream that had trickled down the southern boundary of the town was made its southern limit, and the adjacent parish of All Saints was given a small river frontage and a strip of land to assist its own development.

This change led to the old town being effectively enlarged but still with the original bridge at its centre, with its own church on the bridge, but with a new church on its southern boundary. Several small breweries were constructed and land was made available for shops and a market hall. Some small schools were also built, and then a public reading room. A group of buildings were built which included the public house next to the new masonic hall, and the office of the prominent newspaper of the town.

The masonic fraternity consisted mainly of the brewers and tradesmen, and several of these citizens were also members of the Town Council, who in turn elected its aldermen and the mayor. This small group controlled all aspects of governance of this riverside community.

Chapter 1

ARRIVAL

It was on a fine spring morning on a day towards the end of the nineteenth century that a tall man, with a tanned appearance and wearing a new black clerical suit, descended from the London train at the terminus of the newly-built railway station. This little community on the river showed itself with a burst of clear sunshine as if to greet the candidate for the leadership of the local Methodist church. He, in turn, was impressed by the beauty and tranquillity of this little river community, showing itself at its best for his arrival. The Reverend Bertram Moorehouse had asked for a typical town as a base for his parochial circuit on his return to England from the post in India, where he had performed his missionary duties in a small village situated fifty miles inland from Madras. Here he had married Emma, the beautiful daughter of a minister in the adjoining parish, and together they had brought up two daughters, Alice and Florence, now aged seventeen and fifteen. So far the sisters had been educated alongside the other children of his parish in the mission school which had been near to the Indian village.

The girls had started to acquire behavioral traits that their parents felt would make them seem 'native' and less attractive to prospective English husbands. The worried parents of these two blooming girls were also becoming concerned at their isolation. Bertram hoped that his missionary talents could be adapted to a life in England, so he asked the Missionary Society, or rather their senior organiser the Reverend Thomas Grimes, for a posting to a 'polite' English town that would be suitable for his growing daughters. The Society responded positively and he was directed towards this small riverside paradise, whose population was growing rapidly, but whose present minister was moving away. It had seemed ideal.

The Committee that ran the Methodist movement in the town had a dilemma following the resignation of their leader. This previous incumbent, who had some engineering experience, had been prominent in the establishment of several improvements in the town and was now to move on to become Inspector of locks for the River Authority. The Committee were well aware of the respect that had been earned by this man for the prominent improvements he had introduced and now they were looking for someone who could make a similar impact. The committee was being encouraged to approve the appointment of a new man suggested by the National Methodist Organisation in London. Mr. Chapman, the church committee chairman, was a leading businessman in the town and owner of the largest clothing and haberdashery shop. His well-made suit reflected the wide range from the menswear section of his shop; his fine waistcoat was fronted by a heavy gold chain and a large gold hunter watch. Edwin Chapman frequently consulted this token of his prosperity with a little flourish to rearrange the gold chain. Other members of the selection committee consisted of two mature ladies who had also retired from service in India, dressed in shades of lavender and grey decorated with pretty embroidered flowers. Both wore tasteful black jet necklaces worn out of respect for the Queen. These ladies had been nurses together in a missionary hospital and combined their small savings to buy a home together when they retired. Mr. Clegg, the undertaker from the premises next door – marked with a prominent display of stone crosses and elaborate headstones – and also the caretaker for the church, had a seat on the selection board. Another chair was left empty for Mr. Frith, a generous contributor to the church, who had paid for the bell tower that fronted it. This prominent construction reached towards the sky and was topped with a large bell. It faced the masonic lodge on the other side of the road and gave out its loud message every Sunday. This benefactor was rarely seen in church since he ran a successful legal practice in London, but even when he did visit the town he remained on his estate. This ran along the north side of the town, thus restricting development in that direction. He was, nevertheless, a generous donor to several charities in town and had employed Mr. Climand, a self-made builder and Temperance supporter, in the early stages of that gentleman's building career to construct a gothic lodge and gates at the entrance of his property. Today Mr. Frith was too busy in his office to attend the interview.

'Let's get started then,' said Chairman Chapman. 'The candidate was on the train, I suppose. Call him in please, Mr. Clegg.'

The interview by the Church Council proceeded well and the candidate was feeling pleased with himself. After serving in the Methodist Ministry for the best part of twenty years in India, Bertram Moorehouse was delighted that the recognition of his faithful service to the Church could be rewarded with the possibility of the position of minister in charge of the Methodist congregation of this pleasant and prosperous English town. Bertram now felt that there would be better opportunities for the future education of his two daughters.

The appreciative glances that some of the ship's officers had given to these two girls on their voyage home confirmed the suspicions of their parents and, in turn, these concerns were expressed to the London Office who were sympathetic to Bertram's request to be returned to England. At that time, the Methodist church was considering the spiritual care of wealthy men and women who were looking for new homes in England after a lifetime of service in the outer regions of the Empire. Bertram was an ideal candidate to lead one of these swelling communities. The cities of Bath and London had attracted many of these genteel retired imperial employees, with Brighton and Eastbourne also claiming their share. The town to which Bertram had been invited for interview had also taken trouble to enhance its attractiveness to these wealthier returnees.

It had not been easy to reply to the questions posed by Chairman Chapman who had asked, 'How the candidate would increase the prestige of the Church in the town?' and 'How would the candidate show the superiority of Methodist teaching over that of the other Churches in the area?'

These were unexpected directions for the questioning to take, but Bertrand realised that this reasoning came from the considerable prestige that the previous Methodist minister had obtained for the church in the eyes of the inhabitants of the town. They had benefitted from his construction of a counterbalanced bucket system by which the slope of the road down the hill leading to the town bridge had been reduced. His interest in civil engineering matters had led to his providing advice and a plan for the improvement of the approach road to the bridge. Previously, the hill leading to the bridge had been so steep that a carter and team of four horses had been kept at the bottom to assist anyone with a heavy load wishing to tackle the incline, up or down. The minister's solution had been to organise workers to dig a cutting through the summit of the hill and to deposit the spoil at the bottom using a system of counterbalanced buckets. The slope was reduced, the carter was sent into retirement, and the inhabitants were grateful. They were more grateful when it was realised how much extra toll money this improvement raised from travellers who could save fifteen miles from their journey to Oxford. All this had been accomplished by the previous minister alongside his circuit duties; it had made the church much respected and he had created a reputation which was difficult for a successor to emulate.

Bertram replied that of course he would try to increase the respect for the church and he hoped that his efforts would be appreciated, but his own talents had been developed by the saving of souls in India and that 'spiritual' development would be his main aim if he was made a minister in the town. Of course, he would certainly be looking for any other way he could raise awareness of Methodist doctrine and way of living.

The two grey-haired ladies at the end of the table nodded approvingly on hearing this and Mr. Clegg 'harrumphed' approval. Bertram learned later that his lady supporters had spent their careers in India and were already inclined to favour his application for Minister of their church.

Mr. Chapman informed him that the committee needed more time. 'We would like you to go away until after dinner so that we may consider your suitability for the place as Methodist Leader of our community. Then we can tell you our decision.' And he began to write his extensive notes in the Church records as he waved away the other members of the committee. 'We reconvene at two o'clock. Thank you for coming.'

Following his dismissal, Bertram, unsure as to which way to go in a strange town, made his way down to the river, telling himself that he may as well look at its 'wonderful' bridge that had been mentioned. Sure enough, he was impressed by its wide limestone structure and by the decorative carvings which gave it an Italianate appearance. It made an impressive approach to the town from the new hillside road.

Looking over the parapet, Bertram noticed how clear the water seemed to be. For some reason he had expected the water to be coloured by swirling, stirred-up mud. Not at all; the river had a clean greenish appearance with occasional pieces of trailing weed, and it seemed to him to smell fresh. Looking further upstream, his eye was drawn to a part of the water which had been partitioned off by a square of floating logs. This was Old Smithy's swimming place; a further glance showed a neat lawn on the bank with a flower bed in front of a row of huts for changing clothes. A small group of men were splashing about and Old Smithy stood nearby, wearing his naval uniform from days gone by, holding a long wooden pole with a large hook on the end and acting as a life guard.

His experience as a waterman resulted in Old Smithy occasionally being called upon to recover bodies from the weir on instruction from the Council. Today was 'men" day, with tomorrow reserved for 'ladies only.' A close-knit green hedge surrounded the whole area to keep out peepers and nonpayers. School classes had priority for swimming on Mondays so practically everyone in the town had learnt to swim at Smithy's at one time or another.

The river flow had already been improved during the previous century by the installation of a pound lock and weir downstream. This was intended to facilitate the flow of trade goods to the larger conurbations downstream, notably to London. Coincidentally, the increased width of the river gave broad vistas to the large estates on either side of the river, enhancing the views from the adjacent large houses. The town council had further proposed that the river be widened and be straightened for about a mile upstream to an island in the middle of the river. Although the first idea had again been to improve the properties on the town side of the river, it became obvious that what had been created was an ideal straight stretch of water for boat racing. Coincidentally, at that time the Universities of Oxford and Cambridge were looking for a neutral setting for their annual competition and they found this new stretch of the river to be ideal for their purpose. Since then they had held their regatta there every summer. Everyone was satisfied. Surrounding estates had beautiful water vistas which enhanced the panoramas from their homes, and the Council encouraged the increase in the property values of the riverside residences. What is more, extra visitors came to the town to admire these improvements. The arrival of a branch line of the Great Western railway a year or two later, together with the associated hotel built at the terminus, made the town a most convenient area in which to live. Those of a certain affluence came to the town to retire knowing that they could visit their businesses in London and be back later the same day if called upon. This good service was arranged by a director of the GWR who lived a little upriver, who took his breakfast in his dining car each day as he travelled up to the city, and shared a bottle of whisky with likeminded businessmen on the five o'clock return journey.

'This place is becoming a real alternative to Bournemouth,' one councillor was heard to say with a knowing smile.

Bertram made his way to the centre of the bridge and looked at his surroundings, noting the estates with their fine landscaped grounds.

Passers-by paid no attention to a clergyman in a fresh clerical suit admiring the river surroundings, most visitors to the town did the same thing. The gentle flow of water was perfect to encourage peaceful thoughts in the mind of an observer, or for any of the townsfolk who rested by the river bank watching the flow.

'The river flow is a measure of time for the passage of life,' Bertram mused, wondering which classical poet had first sown this thought in his mind.

'I will use that in my first sermon,' he noted mentally.

On looking over the parapet away from the river and towards the town he was surprised to see a crowd gathering, and even more surprised to learn the reason.

The news of the arrival of the elephants had been well gossiped following the procession of a circus around the small streets that morning, and the final parade down the High street. The circus had made its way towards the meadow where the large tent had been erected. A brass band of six musicians had led the way, followed by acrobats, cages of animals, and girls on befeathered horses. Three decorated elephants brought up the rear, wearing big multi-coloured saddle cloths with a little seat for the mahout on the biggest one. Everyone in the town now knew that the circus had arrived.

At dinner time word reached the open door of the National School at the top of the hill that excitement was afoot.

'Sir! Sir!' Peter Groves called through the door of the Maltster's Arms situated conveniently across the school yard, where the schoolmaster spent most of his afternoons.

'There's elephants in the river, can we go for a look?'

'Certainly not!' said the master, taking another swig of the town's best bitter and turning to the barman for confirmation of the justice of his decision, who nodded.

'Get on with your work,' he added.

The distance over the yard was enough for Peter Groves to reinterpret the message into terms he wished to hear so that when he reached the schoolroom the new form of the message was, 'Sir said we can go,' and the classroom emptied. Boys crept down the side of the school hidden from the alehouse and made their way down to the boat yard at the river's edge.

Sure enough, there were the three elephants splashing around in the river and squirting each other with their trunks. They had moved just deep enough to be out of reach of the mahout who already was trying to make them return to the launching slope of the boatyard since his instruction was to be back at the circus tent ready for the first performance that afternoon. The clever animals had ignored that instruction and were determined to enjoy the water for as long as possible with the long hot walk of the morning not yet forgotten. The incomprehensible shouts of the mahout were ignored as were the calls from the growing crowd on the bank and from the boys on the handsome bridge, just upstream from the splash party. As their handler moved towards them, the elephants went deeper into the water, playing what was to them obviously a game.

This sport had turned into quite a little gala for the town with most of the residents now turning up to enjoy the free spectacle which only ended when the mahout returned to the riverside with a supply of apples. The animals allowed themselves to be rounded up by old Higgs, the owner of the local boat yard, in his rowing boat.

The good-humoured crowd moved away, and Bertram, who had enjoyed the spectacle with the rest, walked back to the Church with a reflective smile on his face; one which linked the playful elephant episode with similar memories drawn from the past. The water in those other days was warm and brown, the clothes of the watching crowd were brighter, and Bertram had enjoyed the fun of watching elephants in the river. On previous hot days, his own children had played in the water with the others from the mission. This distant memory was from a country a long way off, but it showed him once more that people are much the same all over the world, with the same search for simple fun and happiness. He wondered perhaps he could use this little episode in a sermon.

At the afternoon session Mr. Chapman announced to Bertram, 'We like your approach to things and we think that there's a lot you could offer our community, so we want you to join us here. This is subject to two things. First you must let your wife and girls see the town and the manse to know that they will be happy here. Second, we want you to understand how things are run in this town.'

'Get to know the people and help them in their search for a better life.'

'You will know that we have a Mayor and a Council but division here is not a political one, not at all. The town is divided into those who support the brewery, and this group consists mainly of Freemasons who all attend St Mary's church near the bridge, and then there is the Temperance group that attends All Saints church which although nominally in the next parish is really in the south side of the town. Our Methodist church is situated right on the boundary between the two C of E parishes and right opposite the Freemason's lodge. Please make yourself familiar with the way things work here, but do not forget we are wholly behind the Temperance Brigade here.'

He then went on to describe how a year or two previously, when the leading builder and strong Temperance supporter, Mr. Climand, had visited the House of Lords to give evidence for the new Licensing Act, he had disclosed to their Lordships that the number of brewery outlets or alehouses in the town was one in every six houses, which he claimed led to uncontrolled drunkenness. While he was away, someone burnt his builder's yard down to the ground. It was whispered that the young son of the brewery owner, Rupert Brandish, had stood by the fire and ranted, 'What a shame that old Temperance demon was not on top of his pyre.' And as the yard blazed away, the town fire brigade watched.

'You see that we have our troubles here,' said the chairman. 'But I trust that from now our Methodists will be part of the solution.' To which Bertram nodded vigorously.

'Well then, let's get you settled in.'

'God bless you all.' Bertram said to the committee who all seemed pleased with their choice.

Chapter 2

THE NEW EDITOR

The move to the manse was smooth, with the number of chests and boxes fitting well around the heavy furniture the church had provided in the substantial building. The three floors had adequate fittings for a family of four, and the housekeeper-cum-cook, Mrs. Dorkins, had an attic room which still left other loft space for the travelling trunks. The accommodation for the girls looked meagre, but they did not seem to notice the lack of chairs and dressing tables.

'Do you know, Mama, that here we have one room each?'

Surprise showed in the excited tone of this discovery by the two delighted souls who had recently had to share a cabin on the journey from India. Mr. Chapman had played a large part in increasing the comfort of the manse by supplying some reasonably-priced material which Mrs. Dorkins had made into pretty curtains for each room. The owner of the Emporium had also found a few choice pieces of second-hand furniture to help the family settle comfortably into their large house in a short time. Finally, a little housemaid was employed to help Mrs. Dorkins. Emma ticked off the inventory that came with the home and examined her domain each day with a contented smile. Bertram again noticed the graceful movements that had attracted him to her in their early days as he watched her pat her new cushions into place as though she had made some new friends. This contentment was noticed by the members of the church with whom he had dealings, and smiles replaced the stress lines caused by the move as Bertram's sense of humour returned. So, on Sunday, he was able to mention the episode of the elephants in the river as an omen of being welcomed from India into the town congregation.

The large mahogany table in the dining room was suitable for eight people but when laid up for four for dinner it still looked splendid, even without any real silver. Bertram used each evening family meal as a time for hearing all of the news of the day. The two girls bubbled over, each trying to tell their father of all the things they had seen, one often correcting the other when reporting the same event. Everything was new to them and they were especially amazed by all of the tempting items in the shops, and by the bustle of the market. Alice made a special mention of any item of ladies' clothing that caught her notice.

'And do you know Papa that there is one shop that sells real diamond jewelry?'

'And Papa, everything is so green,' added Florence, whose eyes had traced the surrounding hills.

Emma had spent most of the first day enquiring after suitable schools and certainly the town had the new schools prescribed for its children by the fairly recent Education Act. These had been built by Mr. Climand, the local builder in the town, who had offered the lowest tender. Located in the centre of the town and with the proscribed separate entrances labelled 'Boys' and 'Girls', it gave free education to all local children who in the past may have had only a rudimentary teaching in the town's Church Schools. Mr. Chapman had, however, rather recommended the private establishment for the girls run by Miss McGregor, taking only a few girls aged between twelve and eighteen who, when they emerged, were expected to enter local society into which they later married. This establishment could be found slightly up the hill, just past the police station, and Emma had spent most of the morning talking to Miss McGregor and her French assistant to see if it was suitable. She was finally persuaded of the school's quality when she learnt of its reputation for the training of singing voices, something she had always wanted for herself.

'I am sure you both will be able to find some nice friends there and they will tell you all about the town. Of course, you will also learn music and French amongst your other lessons.'

Going from the school room to the quiet area, Miss McGregor turned to Emma and said softly 'We have very high standards here for the girls and we are usually full, but one reason that there is a space for your family is because recently I had to let a girl go.' Then she continued in a whisper, 'She was expecting a baby by a servant up at the Hall and we can't have that you know. This is a very proper establishment!'

Emma nodded in agreement.

That evening, Mrs. Dorkins prepared a special welcoming meal, using delicacies from the market place. A soup, made from freshly-gathered field mushrooms was well received, but the poached bream with leeks did not please girlish tastes more used to Indian spices.

Roasted leg of veal in a rich brown sauce with potatoes satisfied everyone, but not before Bertram had checked with the cook to make sure that no Madeira had been used in its preparation, and Mrs. Dorkins had given an affirmatory nod. She also explained the delicious red berry sponge pudding had been made from mulberries gathered from a local garden. There were several mulberry trees around the area dating from an earlier failed attempt to grow silk worms with which to start a new industry. Unfortunately, the trees did not suit silk worms but remained in place for their berries to be used in the town's kitchens. A vote by the family members on which cuisine they preferred was three to one in favour of English over Indian fare, and Mrs. Dorkins smiled as she saw that her work was appreciated.

When they had finished their evening meal and the dishes were cleared, Emma went through the details of her visit to the school, concluding that it seemed to be a very proper establishment. On their first visit to the Academy, Emma had handed over her daughters to Miss McGregor, the owner of the establishment, who had then introduced a senior pupil, of a similar age to Alice, and then a younger girl who was more like Florence. The four went off to explore the building and schoolrooms.

'We are quite a select group here, you know, and only take girls above twelve. And by the time they are eighteen, they are finished very nicely,' Miss McGregor told Emma.

'I have a French maid who teaches the language and I look after English. Writing and the Classics are our main subjects, with enough sums to teach the girls about money.'

When the girls spoke of their day and mentioned that they had all joined the singing class in the afternoon, Emma was satisfied that her offspring would eventually turn into two attractive, well balanced young ladies and on hearing of the school visit Bertram was equally pleased. He had not expected the town to be so refined and he looked forward to seeing his two 'gems' shine in this superior environment.

'Did you like it, girls?' he asked. 'Sounds perfect to me.' But both girls looked apprehensive.

'You will love it when you've settled in,' Emma told them, and of course they did.

At subsequent evening meal times Bertram heard their daily stories and these confirmed that the decision had been the right one.

'Today we sang *Summer is icumen in*,' they told their father.

'Loudly sing cuckoo,' Bertram sang, reminded of his own schooldays.

Later he was to look forward to the girl's daily news as it usually linked into other gossip of the town.

'Papa, all of the trees on the hills are turning orange and red,' Florence said one evening. 'And it makes the river looked orange as well. Did you see it yet?'

At another time near to Christmas, 'Papa, the street in front of the Coach House is full of geese!' Alice noted.

'And some of them have tar on their feet,' added Florence.

'They've probably walked a long way to the Christmas market,' their father explained. 'Tomorrow, I expect you'll see the pigs go to the bidding ring behind the Public House.'

'Can we go to see the sale?' They chorused.

'Well, perhaps, if you can clean your shoes afterwards. But remember your efforts after animal sales in India. Not very thorough, as I recall.' That was the end of that suggestion.

'We went to the town school's carol concert at St Mary's today. All the children in the town went. Was that the right thing for us to do?'

'Of course it was. Isn't it the church that Miss McGregor attends?'

'Yes. Mr. Climand wished us Merry Christmas; he's a churchwarden there.'

'And he asked us to pass on his best wishes to our parents,' Florence added.

This was well noted by Bertram, who gave Emma a knowing wink.

Both his daughters liked to tell their father of the news of the day that had caught their attention, sometimes competing for his hearing. Bertram enjoyed this part of the day which he thought was an ideal feature of family life. Each day, something different, he mused.

In February, Alice told her father, 'Did you know, Papa, that now the meadows are frozen some boys skated all the way from the lower lock through the town up to the island?'

'I didn't realise it was frozen so far, but the water is less deep along the boat racing course which makes the water easier to chill and freeze.'

Spring arrived and with it the thaw in the meadows.

Later in the year, 'There were cows back in the meadows this morning, Papa. We will be able to walk along the river bank on Sunday afternoon,' Florence reported.

After a short period of a month or so, Bertram looked back with some wonder to the series of events that had led to his becoming a spiritual leader in this prosperous little riverside town. On consideration, he thought that he and his family were becoming accepted by his flock and that each day he was becoming more familiar with the make-up of the town community.

His attempt to become accepted had been given a considerable helping hand by an offer from a member of his congregation. Later he looked back at this event with disbelief, and even now he looked at himself with surprise as he realised that he had become the owner and editor of one of the town newspapers: *The Advertiser*.

This gift from above had come to pass one day in May as he was strolling through the town on his return walk after paying a visit to an elderly Church member. A spark of inspiration struck as he gazed through the shop window of the local chemist and he noticed the owner beckoning him into the store. Mr. Butler was one of his congregation, and today he had an urgent look on his face.

'Do you have a minute or two to talk a bit of business?' the chemist asked as he crooked his finger at Bertram. Butler's business was mainly the supply of potions and ointments prescribed by the town doctors for the maintenance of the health of the population, and he had several flagons of coloured water in his window to advertise the fact. But he also owned the smaller of the two newspapers in the town, *The Advertiser*. Mr. Butler was seventy and wanted to pass on his affairs to his son, who was already a qualified pharmacist but lived in in Oxford. No problem existed with the chemist's shop and potion business, but his son did not have time to run a little local paper. In fact, he still intended to live in Oxford with his family, employing a local manager here in the town. As his son did not want to take on the burden of the newspaper, Mr. Butler wished to sell his interest in it.

'It more or less runs itself,' he told Bertram. 'There's Mrs. Pilling who runs the office and takes the advertisements, and we have a young man to lay out the pages which we send to the next town to the Berkshire Press, who print the copies on their spare capacity and send them back on the train. We have got paperboys who then deliver them around the area to our subscribers. You would need to write some editorial material once a month but you could use the paper to carry one of your amusing sermons, like the one about the elephants, or make some other church points, or put in a monthly prayer, anything, so long as it does not promote beer!' He finished with a knowing wink.

'I'm sure you are aware of the friction that exists between Climand and the Brandish family but you might not know of the incident during the campaign for the representative for the new County Council a year or two back. Feelings were very bad then because the new Council had the power to grant beer licenses for the town, which had previously been in the power of the Town Council, and these had always been turned down. Rightly so, if you consider how many public houses we have here. There was much free beer offered on polling day and Brandish became our County Councillor. But during the celebrations in the evening, his supporters carried a rowing boat around the town full of free beer, and there was a lot of singing and shouting going on. Especially outside Climand's house. The crowd didn't know that Climand's younger son, Lawrence, was dying of the fever until he opened his door and asked for some quiet and respect for his boy. The crowd moved down to the riverside but the damage had been done. Brandish and Climand have been sworn enemies ever since.'

He continued, 'Be very careful what you write about those two. But,' he restated, 'the advertising pays very well.'

Bertram had become quite excited, for he could see a number of his ambitions being satisfied with this one move into the newspaper business.

If it made a little money it would help his stipend and contribute to the approaching expenses of his blossoming family. On his way to England, he had not thought about his growing daughters, but their development was now being brought firmly to his attention and he had already realised that he and his family had a certain position to keep up in the society of this small town. The acquisition of the newspaper started to suggest all sorts of opportunities to Bertram as he turned the suggestion over in his mind. The paper could be the answer to his pending financial awkwardness! In addition, there was the possibility of using *The Advertiser* as a banner for the Church, which would help boost its prestige as mentioned to him during his interview with the Committee. He was warming to the idea of editorship.

He then went upstairs to the office above the shop to meet his potential employees, who assured him that the running of the paper was very smooth, and that they looked forward to some interesting stories from him to liven it up and make their work more interesting. Bertram went down the stairs and finished agreeing with Mr. Butler a price for the paper, to be paid in instalments as the income from circulation made possible.

When he told Emma of his fortuitous purchase of the newspaper, Bertram experienced very little resistance. His excitement showed in his face, and Emma became infected by it when she thought of the opportunities the new purchase offered. The possibility to make an indelible impression for the Church on the town was also very clear to her, so she agreed readily with her husband.

'This must be an ideal way to expand the message of the Church. Perhaps a little homily each month surrounded by touches of local news. Births, marriages, and deaths always need announcements,' he told her.

Emma put her arms around her husband and looked into his eyes.

'This is the way forward.' She smiled at him, giving him an encouraging kiss.

Chapter 3

TOWN AFFAIRS

During the next weeks Bertram discovered that people he met could be characterised by which of the other two Churches they attended and this was mostly determined by which part of the town they lived in. The old part of the town contained traditional businesses and shops in addition to the main parish church of St Mary with its surrounding schools, markets, and the last remaining brewery, owned by the Brandish family. There were also people living near to the Town Hall in courtyards where the homes of several families could be found crowded together. These people often shared a dwelling and they sometimes had lodgers in their homes as well. Frequently there was only one water tap and one toilet per courtyard. Market traders drew their labourers from this enclave and the surrounding estates found their domestic staff from the labour pool there.

Many of the town businesses relied for their income on the large estates that surrounded the town and they frequently visited the big houses with a pony and trap to exhibit their wares, always visiting by the back door or tradesmen's entrance. The town could probably have been considered as a prosperous service town just for its surrounding Big House business but the local entrepreneurs made even more money from the flow of visitors who now arrived by train for day trips, or for the fishing, or for the annual rowing regatta. Bertram found a mine of little stories from all of these sources with which to fill his publication and these in turn brought in advertising. By the time spring had arrived he no longer worried about his daughter's dresses for the summer and he even considered buying a Panama hat for himself.

'Fashionable, but a trifle dandyish,' he mused, seeing himself in a mirror.

As Bertram became more familiar with its layout he noticed more and more improvements being made to the town.

These further town developments included a sewage farm built to replace collections by the night soil men, and this new facility was placed downriver. Further up the valley where the main road led to Oxford, the Council agreed to the construction of a rifle practice range where young men of the local Yeomanry were drilled and taught firing skills in safety. This was in preparation for the call for the local regiment to go and face the Boers when needed.

The south of the town had been designated to be part of the parish of All Saints, with a small river frontage for their commercial needs, but the brewery owned by the Grey family had recently been merged with Brandish interests and much of the meadowland to the south was ready for urban expansion. Until recently the ownership of these land plots had been challenged by individuals who owned ancient ground deeds. A shrewd town clerk, who was also a masonic officer, had collected the old deeds together and bound them into one land ownership document which was sold to raise town funds to a single development company owned by several local builders. Thus, the land to the south of the town was being developed for new housing. The strip of land from All Saints Church down to the river was traded to Mr. Climand in exchange for his constructing two new chancel extensions to the church. After this addition, the expanded church warranted the appointment of an additional curate and this post was filled by the appointment of the Reverend Palmer, a vigorous young priest with a strong Temperance background.

The Methodist church had purchased a fine plot on the main road leading south from the town and a similar piece of land was obtained by the Masons. The flow of families into the newly constructed properties became part of the new water company's plan to install a piped fresh water system and this was linked to a new water tower built at the northern edge of the old town on land sold by Mr. Frith the Methodist lawyer. Shortly afterwards the expansion of the gasworks occurred and they buried their new supply pipelines to the newly built houses. Mr. Climand and the other builders were ready to erect rows of cheap houses and some villas to satisfy this need and Bertram arranged for his paperboys to leave a free copy of the *Advertiser* whenever they noticed a freshly occupied home. Bertram had arranged for a rather splendid engraving of the Methodist Church to be placed prominently on the front page of the paper with a welcoming sentence. He observed that this inflow of commercial activity acted as a stimulus to attendance at the Methodist Church and it seemed that the families of the water managers and gas engineers preferred his more open and friendly form of service. This was according to his plan, but other Methodists were not so ready to give the *Advertiser* credit for the increase in numbers. Other small businesses came to the town from other areas and the high street became a thriving commercial centre. Each new arrival brought managers and staff, all of whom required places to live and they moved into the newly built suburb. Bertram discovered that the new families appreciated the comfort of a visit from welcoming clergy and he made special efforts to visit them.

Emma noticed a change in her husband's demeanor at each evening meal whenever he returned from his editorial duties. He was frequently ready with a funny story if he had heard one during his tour of the town businesses. In fact, she discovered that her husband had become quite a popular character willing to chat to anybody who had a few moments to spare. Bertram, 'call me Bertie,' he often said, mentioned to his wife that he considered his editorial stroll to be promotion of the Methodist cause in the best way possible, particularly as he had become a strong supporter of the Temperance movement. This, of course, contrasted with the ideas promoted by *The Standard* owned by the Blandish brewery and the town group of Masons, which were considered dull, and the vicar of St Mary's, their church representative, found it difficult to maintain the same pace as his younger rival in the attraction of souls.

Emma had also found a role to play in the town during her stroll home after escorting the girls to Miss McGregor's academy each morning.

'I will be walking with you to school,' Emma told her girls on their first day. 'This will give me a chance to see something of the town.' It also gave her time to look in many of the shop windows, an occupation she enjoyed, as she secretly wanted to look at the establishment of

Mr. Chapman, the Methodist church leader, to gain an insight as to the type of man he was. After all, in his position, he could be a big influence in their lives.

The Chapman Emporium had three windows facing on to the main shopping street of the town, each displaying goods according to the main shop division within – haberdashery, men's clothes, and ladies' fashions. The latter interested Emma the most and she gave a casual glance over the various items until she noticed from behind the display the hand of Mr. Chapman himself beckoning her inside.

'Come in,' he mouthed, and pointed to the door.

'What do you think of the display?' he asked her. 'Don't you think it's rather splendid? Did you notice the Indian silks? They've just arrived.'

Emma had indeed noticed these rolls of material in the centre of the display and made the appropriate murmur of approval without mentioning that they were beyond her purse.

'Let me show you the rest of the store. I'm sure you've noticed the wide range of products we sell here and we try to supply all the needs of the ladies in the town. As a matter of fact, we also supply many of the surrounding estates. Anything from servants' uniforms to ball gowns,' Mr. Chapman said, grandly, conveniently omitting the fact that the upper strata actually purchased their finer items of clothing when they visited their town houses in London, but giving the impression that he clothed several beauties at the County events. And he continued in this vein as they toured the whole store. Emma was particularly interested in the overhead wire system which conveyed little pots of money from the sales counters to the cash desk which sent the receipt and change whizzing back to the appropriate counter along the overhead wires to where the sales assistant was serving the customer.

'You approve of our modern system I see,' the owner said.

The tour continued throughout the whole store with Emma responding appropriately, occasionally being really impressed by the range of things sold and sometimes with genuine interest in a new item she had not seen before.

At the end of the tour, Chapman said, with an air of mystery, 'Come up to my office and I will order up some tea for us. You can rest yourself and there is something I wish to say to you.' They were already on the first floor and they passed by the better-quality gowns and ladies accessories to enter the office marked 'Private' at the rear.

'I do not wish to offend you, but I have a problem here that I wish to discuss and on which I would appreciate your opinion,' the store owner said as they sipped their Orange Label Ceylon tea provided by his secretary, and Emma nodded for him to explain as she continued drinking.

'As you are new to the town you may not know that I am an Alderman here and one day I may be the Mayor.' Pause for breath as the news was absorbed.

'This makes it difficult sometimes for me to control the business as I would like. What is more,' here Chapman's face started to flush a little, 'I am sometimes uncomfortable in this side of my business for I think that a man should not be here to advise ladies'…more reddening…,'on their garments.' Here, a little sigh of relief. He continued, 'Since we met, I've noticed your natural poise and elegance and I've been wondering if you could help me now that I'm unable to be here as often as I would wish.'

It was clearly good for him to have reached this far, as his colour faded to pale pink. Emma sipped some more tea wondering what Chapman really wanted to say.

'What I have in mind is for you to come to the Emporium once or twice a week, if you have time, when I am involved with town work, and talk to any ladies here about their dress needs, etcetera, etcetera, to help them choose what they can from our stock. You will not have to sell anything; our assistants will do that. What I would like is for you to put them at their ease and introduce new fabrics to them. More like friendly advice, etcetera, and etcetera. What do you think of this idea?' He hurriedly added, 'of course any Church work where you might be needed would come first.' Emma hummed to herself as she absorbed this offer which had come so unexpectedly.

'I would not think of offering you money; that would not do at all. What I have in mind is perhaps that you could help me at this very busy time and I could give you an account and perhaps some sort of stipend at the year-end.'

He went on, 'If you would like to try on some of the new dress arrivals at any time, I have a very comfortable ladies' sitting room and changing facility you could use.'

This was all a surprise to Emma and she did not immediately say 'Yes,' but gave a smile of understanding and said that of course she must discuss this with Bertram.

After dinner Bertram listened to everything and, while he hoped Emma would look after the ladies who arranged flowers and dusted in the Church, and give them a tea-party from time to time, said he had no objections. In fact, he was pleased for Emma to perform these small favours for a senior member of the church committee. When Mr. Chapman told Bertram of his proposal, the latter gave the impression he was surprised, but indicated that he approved.

The following day Chapman quietly mentioned that. 'If this little plan works out well I will show my appreciation to

Emma at the end of the year if she would accept it.' Bertram nodded assent.

This encouraged another smile. Thus, a regular routine developed for Emma who enjoyed her walk to the school with her daughters after which she made her way to the Emporium on Tuesdays and Thursdays for chats with her new-made friends about dresses and such in the ladies' clothes section. Chapman arranged a special chair for her near to the entrance from where she could recognise future clients and where she could guide wives from the town and surrounding estates towards the latest clothes and fashions.

Wednesday was half-day closing and Friday a cattle market day, and nobody shopped on Mondays. On these days she often visited the Temperance Coffee rooms which were situated behind the main shopping street and where she saw Church members. Emma found that single ladies, especially widows from the colonies, did not like to use the rest room facilities offered by the other businesses in the town as they were invariably near to public alehouses so these special clients preferred to rest in Emma's sitting room in the shop. Bertram was amused by the development. It often gave him an ear to any gossip in the town after his evening meal. He really felt that the family were settling in very well indeed. He was also very pleased with the way his daughters had made friends at school and their efforts with the singing class pleased him enormously.

In his first few weeks of his position as Methodist Minister Bertram had made the acquaintance of as many of the inhabitants as he could; he started to like and understand this pleasant town to which he and his family had moved. He became familiar with the Haberdashers and Clothiers Emporium of Mr. Chapman at the crossroads, and with the several public houses selling Brandish beers and ales, none of which did he enter. He did go into the Temperance Coffee House, greeting several of his parishioners in the process.

On one of his tours he noted with interest the square front of the new town hall with the plaque reminding visitors of the laying of the foundation stone by Mr. Smith, the National Newsagent. Another notice with the square and compasses of the Masonic Lodge recorded the fact that the stone had been laid with the blessing of the Masonic Deputy High Priest. Bertram had read of this event in the *Standard*, which listed the masonic title of every significant politician in the town, and also that the event had been organised by the mayor, Dr. Redesdale. The report finished with a description of the children's party held in the mayor's garden.

Many of these young people knew the doctor well as he paid them sixpence each for the vials of poppy juice they collected from the half-acre of poppy flowers behind his surgery, juice which he converted into laudanum. Bertram discovered that as well as being a chief mason, Dr. Redesdale was the current Mayor and the prime organiser of the finance for new Town Hall.

Not present at this celebration was the builder, and previous Alderman, Mr. Climand, who remained at his yard next to the Town Hall which still showed the blackened scars of the fire the previous year. The enmity between Mr. Climand and the Brandish brewers was described to Bertram several times during his tour, as a snippet of scandal which the parishioner thought 'B' should know. A witness told him too that the fire brigade took half an hour to cross the street to extinguish the flames, which they only did when the fire threatened the pub next door to the blazing yard.

'But Climand could not call the brigade because he was in London at that time giving evidence to the House of Lords Committee who were considering changes to the

Licensing Laws, and where he gave evidence that the town had one of the highest proportions of public houses per head of population in the country.' This admission had roused the anger of the town authorities who did not approve of this fact being widely known. They countered that the local police rarely had to make arrests for drunkenness, unless personal violence occurred. No mention was made that at that time the local constabulary was appointed by the Council. This power was to change with the new licensing laws drawn up by Parliament as a result of the Lords enquiry.

Bertram returned home and quietly absorbed what he had learnt. He had been told that Mr. Climand had purchased the stone from the demolished old town hall, and had re-erected it on a plot in the next county, which he now used as his son's and his own family residence. On a later tour, Bertram made a special visit to the Climand Yard where he noticed that the remaining building still had blackened traces of gothic windows, decorative tiling, and elaborate doorways which had originally been used to demonstrate the artistic possibilities for future clients and which could have been added to any future Climand new construction.

'This town is a lot more complicated than I first thought,' he confided to Emma after dinner. As was now common at the Manse dinner table, nothing too serious was discussed during the family evening meal so after desert and seeing four empty plates, Bertram would nod to Mrs. Dorkins who stepped forward to clear the table and the family passed to the drawing room next door. Each member was eager to tell the others the excitements of the day, but Bertram refrained from telling the detail of his discovery of the masonic power in the town in front of the children. He was overcome by his daughters as the two girls hurried into their places bubbling over to give all the details of their day at the Academy for Girls. Bertram's smile told the family of his pleasure and he thought all this excitement to be a very good sign.

The following day, Miss McGregor took Emma to one side and suggested that the girls might like to mix a little more with the young people and that it might be a good idea for them to join the Temperance Choir.

'I myself am a member of the St Mary's group who make up the altos.' Miss McGregor had proudly added and she had hinted that Alice and Florence might like to see some of the other singers at the choir rehearsals. She would introduce them and accompany them to rehearsals in the Assembly rooms, and bring them home afterwards if necessary. Both children had lovely voices and would enjoy singing a more serious type of music with different parts sung by members of some of the other choirs in the area. They would also be able to meet the Reverend Palmer who, as curate for All Saints Church, was their choirmaster. Rehearsals were on Thursday evenings except when a concert was near when they were increased to two or three evenings a week.

Bertram thought this was excellent, both for the girls who loved singing and for the wider image it gave of the Methodists being part of the community. Alice and Florence thought it would be splendid to be singing four-part music with tenors and basses – and altos of course. They were part of the combined choir who led the carol concert at St Mary's with proud mama and papa in the congregation of the big town church. The vicar came over and shook Bertram's hand afterwards and wished him a Holy Christmas. All things taken together, Bertram thought that the move back to England had been as good as they had hoped, and when he smiled towards Emma and when she smiled in return, he felt truly blessed.

Chapter 4

TRAGEDY

It was on a dull day in late March that Miss McGregor had emerged from her private quarters into the schoolroom looking very pale and her voice trembling as she gathered her pupils around her desk.

'I have some terrible news, girls, and I am so upset that I do not think we will be having lessons today.' Her puzzled listeners looked at each other for an explanation, but no one knew what the matter was.

'Some of you will remember Mary, Mary Grey, who was a pupil here recently, a pretty girl and good with her needle and a nice singing voice too. Well she has been shot by her father. It was not an accident because her father and mother are also dead.'

Gasps...and then tears. Miss McGregor herself could not speak for a few seconds. The coachman, with the gamekeeper and parlour maids, had just driven to the police station which was near to the school and Miss McGregor had been asked by the police sergeant to take care of the young maids, who were almost hysterical. From these she had learnt that the cook had also been shot. None of the witnesses knew when the killings had taken place, and certainly no one knew why.

Something terrible had occurred within the Grey family during the previous evening, something so unexpected that those who were told could not credit it. Later the town newspaper attempted to guess the details and a magistrate's enquiry held a week later was none the wiser. There appeared to be no reason for this tragedy.

All the crucial facts centred on local business deals involving Major Grey, a military man on half-pay, attached to the local Bucks Yeomanry.

'Always ready to be recalled if those Boers gave any more trouble,' and 'Primed for action when needed,' he'd often told his friends – and anyone else who would listen.

Grey's father had been the owner and operator of the second largest brewery in the town, or just outside of the town to be accurate. Since the parish boundaries had been laid out, the adjacent parish had been given a small river frontage which had facilitated the running of a small brewery, whose products were sold throughout the town as well as in the wider area of villages nearby. The small wharf enabled the Grey brewery to import the malt it needed by river and to send a proportion of its brewing to other river locations. At his decease, his father had left the business to his only son, who was then forced to resign his full army commission to sort things out. The business demanded all of his attention, it being somewhat run down and in need of capital, and this was at a time when several other needy ancient cousins were requesting their portions.

A solution presented itself to the Major when Percy Brandish, the managing director of Brandish Beers and

Ales, the other town brewery, made a substantial offer for the whole of Grey's business. This offer included the offer of a directorship of a related brewery in London, in which Brandish had a minority interest. It also carried the tenancy of a small manor house for the Grey family just outside of the town, and which was a short distance above the Brandish residence next to their town brewery. A watching brief over the London business was offered to Grey as part of the deal but it necessitated his travelling up to town several times a week. This was not disagreeable to Major Grey because he had heard of the fast train service for businessmen. The line had recently been modernised with the section from the town being laid on the new standard gauge track, enabling a fast, non-stop service to the junction with the GWR main line to town. First class carriages with a restaurant car were provided and, if it was desired, one could purchase a full breakfast at the journey's start and finish it comfortably before one's arrival. This service, known locally as 'The Flyer,' was instigated by the GWR director who lived in the town and who ran this service to suit his own demanding standards and needs.

The planned sale of the Grey business received the full approbation of Eleanor, the major's wife, and his blossoming daughter Mary, who would not only have the prestige of living on an estate property adjacent to the Brandish home but also a privileged entry into a wide circle of new friends. In addition, the fashionable shops in the nearby towns offered everything a County lady could desire, with the major's transport being available during most days for this purpose. Life was made easier with the employment of a cook/housekeeper and two housemaids who lived locally.

The Grey family status was underscored when they were invited to the party at the bigger brewery for the opening of its new artesian well. Every one of importance in the area was there to be greeted and entertained by the whole Brandish family. Possibly this was where Mary Grey and Rupert Brandish met for the first time, maybe he showed her around the modernised facilities, who knows, fate has its own way of deciding things. Major Grey began to realise how the acquisition of the estate had changed his status in the area, particularly with the contacts he made with some of the other estate owners he met each morning in the First-Class railway carriage. The new, fast Great Western 'Flyer' had drawn these gentlemen together and several common business interests were discussed on the journey to Paddington. But it was the shared bottle of whisky on the return journey that encouraged this group to bond together. Conversation on these return journeys would often be about the stock market, banks, insurance matters – and promising hints for monetary advantage were confidentially shared.

It was at some time during one of these journeys that Major Grey heard a whisper of the link between the Brandish business and that of the brewery downstream. This bigger business had just installed a new bottling plant for the production of their Empire Pale Ale; brewed for the Colonies. As the market was huge, the project needed malt and hops so that volumes could be maximised. The merger had been discussed between the two brewery owners, who also believed a romantic link existed between young Rupert Brandish and Dorothy Mathey – the handsome only daughter of the brewery owner in the adjacent town who was only slightly older than Rupert. The minds of the two fathers worked together and came to the same conclusion: a merger between the companies would bring huge advantages to both parties.

The joining of two families was so obvious that it was

assumed to be going to take place and the details became secondary to the movement of barrels and bottles. The details were whispered in the railway carriage and the friendly stockbroker who travelled in the group reckoned that the value of both businesses could rise by twenty percent. He refilled the glasses on the train to toast the merger, even though the happy couple were unaware of the detailed planning going on behind their backs. The stockbroker placed his finger in front of his lips after he had given the toast, 'Shhhh.'

Grey was smiling to himself as he left the station.

'Evenin' sergeant,' Grey greeted his coachman, an ex-soldier he had known for years.

'Easy home.' And once there the Major went straight to his dressing room to prepare for dinner. This was an occasion that Eleanor his wife and daughter Mary kept as a formal affair, but if the meal was simple it was understood that the cook would finish the serving to allow the two maids to go home early. Both ladies nevertheless looked at their best as the Major sat at the head of the table.

'Have a nice day dear?' he said, as he always did. This was followed by the usual reply, 'Not too bad dear, how about you?'

Then followed an account of domestic chatter like, 'Walking the dogs' or 'Visited the dressmaker,' etc., as the plates were changed between courses.

Then the Major began to light his cigar as the cook started to prepare coffee.

'How about you, Mary, anything special today?' The usually chatty girl had been quiet and this was her opening. But her mother answered quickly, 'Young Rupert Brandish from next door called in for tea this afternoon and I believe Mary does have something to say to you. Rupert wanted to come and see you some time tomorrow and asked if you could send a note to say when it would be convenient.' Grey's ears pricked up.

'What on earth does he want to talk about?' The conversation of earlier that evening on the train raced through his head, speeded up by half a bottle of Bordeaux and a large brandy. 'Shhhh…' it whispered.

Mary, clearly nervous, burst out with, 'We want to get married and he is coming to ask your permission.' Then, 'We want to get married if you will agree…we love each other.'

'What!' the major expostulated. 'What did you say?'

The girl now, with reason, almost incoherent with fear, stammered, 'Rupert and I…want to get married if you will agree…he is heir to the family brewery, you know… aaaand…'

'Stop! I know what Rupert Brandish is. A bounder, that's what!' Giving Major Grey a few moments for his high colour to subside and to regain his breath.

Mary continued, 'But we love each other…and I am going to have his baby.'

The brandy glass fell from her father's hand as he banged the table with his fist.

'You are not.' He was shouting now. 'That you are not!' And in a quieter tone to his wife, 'Who else knows about this?'

'Just Mummy and I,' mumbled the trembling girl.

'Do you know what you have done? Do you? Her father thundered.

Then to his wife, 'You have let this girl destroy several of the principal families in the area. She has ruined their fortunes.'

After taking another breath, he continued, 'The damage

she has done is immeasurable. The name of Grey has been cast into the mud. We are totally destroyed. Well, it shall not happen!'

By this time the Major was standing up and looking at the ceiling.

'Well it shall not happen!' he repeated. 'Wait here,' he commanded.

He then stormed out of the room, returning a minute or two later and in the process of cocking his old military pistol as he entered the room.

'Marry?...*Never!*' he shouted, and before Eleanor could rise from her chair he had reached his daughter, who by now was cringing away from him, and with one practiced movement he put a ball through his daughter's temple.

'Never!' he repeated through the smoke.

As she lurched forward, he turned, reloaded and primed the gun, and with a swing, raised his arm and shot his wife in the head.

'Traitor!' he shouted at the falling lady, and by this time his face was shiny red.

It was only then that he noticed the cook standing frozen with a coffee pot in one hand and a half-filled cup in the other. Grey took two strides towards her, reloading once more.

'I'm so sorry my dear.' As he shot her between the eyes, he muttered, 'You should not have known all this.'

Early next morning the two young maids, who arrived to light the fires and to deliver the breakfasts, found the house unlocked and the evening candles burnt down to their stubs. The kitchen was in disarray, but that was often the case, and nothing seemed very unusual until they reached the dining room. The awfulness of the three bodies of the night before, sprawled in grotesque positions where they had died, drove them screaming out of the house. They were only stopped by the gamekeeper who had left his cottage earlier to investigate a strange gunshot which came from the copse. There he had found Major Grey tipped forward from the log on which he had been sitting with the pistol still in his hand and the back of his head blown off. The sergeant coachman then rushed up to the house where he was met by the distraught maids. After realising that the dining room horror was beyond anything he could do, he pushed the weeping girls into the coach and made his way into town, where all three went into the police station to describe the scene at the house. He could only state that four persons had been shot at their home and that their bodies had been found by the maids that morning. He could tell the officer on duty nothing else or give any reason for the events he had found, leaving the police to discover the reasons for such folly.

When they were together, Bertram asked Emma if she had heard anything more about this terrible event in town gossip, but Emma could not add anything to the basic news, she could only repeat the guesses that Mary had been expecting a baby. 'But whose?' The rumours abounded, and there were several theories, but the police sergeant could find no reason for the killings; certainly it was not a burglary, nor an aggrieved ex-employee. Even the girl's pregnancy was not confirmed.

Later the town newspaper attempted to guess the details but made no progress, and a magistrate's enquiry held a week later was none the wiser. There appeared to be no reason for this tragedy.

On the evening of the tragedy, Bertram asked his girls at dinner if they had picked up any further news from Miss McGregor, but neither could add anything to the basic facts of the morning, so he encouraged them to go to bed early to help them recover from the shock. In his role of editor of the *Advertiser,* he went to his desk to draft a paragraph for the paper, just giving the facts as he knew them and particularly avoiding any speculation concerning the reasons for the tragedy. He merely ascribed the event to the breakdown of a soldier perhaps provoked by the memory of a military event earlier in his career. His competitor also chose to avoid any discussion of motive in their publication and limited their report to Sergeant Greenaway's account from his official record.

All the cruel facts centred on local business deals involving Major Grey, who was always known to be 'primed for action when needed.'

Later, the local magistrates, one of whom was Brandish senior, examined the facts which were clear enough for them to pronounce three murders and a suicide, and gave authority for the burial of the corpses. That of Major Grey, the suicide, was buried in non-consecrated land outside the churchyard and the women were interred in a previously reserved family plot in the cemetery.

What appeared simple to the magistrates did not appear to be at all simple to the inhabitants of the town, and although the name of Rupert Brandish was not mentioned in the coroner's court it certainly was gossiped among the population who wanted to know: 'Why?' 'Why had such a terrible event taken place? What was the reason?'

The gossip was intense in the Temperance Choir, and, as the case was discussed back and forth, the daughters of the Methodist minister learnt how town morals and standards of behaviour evolved. Miss McGregor asked herself, in an undertone so her girls could hear, 'It would have been more discreet if the parents had sent their daughter to her aunt in some other place for Mary to have the baby.' This solution had been chosen for poor Rose Smith, a former pupil of hers. Rose had disappeared to the bigger town downstream for her confinement, and the supposed father, the footman, was dismissed. 'Much more discreet.'

But although not forgotten, no further details emerged. These horrible events passed into memory and the subjects of gossip moved on. The impact of the disgrace remained firmly in the memory of every young woman in the town and their attitude towards single motherhood always remained coloured by the experience of poor Mary and her baby.

Chapter 5

THE PICNIC

It was sometime later in June that excited chatter came from
the door of Alice's bedroom as the two daughters of Reverend
Bertram prepared for the summer picnic organised for the new
Temperance Choir. They had put on their new dresses and
were admiring their reflections in front of the large dressing
table mirror. Florence was brushing her sister's hair while
Alice polished her nails with the chamois leather borrowed
from Mama's manicure set. Emma's thought concerning
a little extra rouge for their cheeks was quickly dismissed in
view of the promised fine weather for the day ahead.

Although he was pleased with the way in which the
Temperance Choir was developing, Reverend Palmer had
believed that a social gathering would bring the group
together. Fortunately, Mr. Frith, the owner of the largest
house near the centre of the town and a strong Temperance
supporter, instantly responded. He would be delighted to
make his garden available for a social occasion if Reverend
Palmer thought it would help.

Frith told his servants to prepare a little tea party for the Temperance Choir on this day in June, which he hoped would be sunny. The gardeners were told to display everything at its best; flower borders to be immaculate, rare plants beautifully displayed, even the paths were to be raked between the shady fern banks. Those who had attended similar occasions in the past warned other choir members that the highest standards of dress and behaviour were expected. The two daughters of the Reverend Moorehouse had risen to the occasion and both had new dresses made out of Indian silk from Chapman's Emporium, which their mother had made up to give a sari-like look. Alice, now eighteen, and Florence, sixteen, both looked very cool and elegant as they carried their new clothes with something of the style they had learnt in India. This was something new for the town.

All went well. Jellies and junkets were consumed, delicate sandwiches and fairy cakes enjoyed, and chilled lemonade sipped daintily – and there were strawberries. Curate Palmer made a speech thanking the absent Mr. Frith (away on business), and his staff. Then the butler replied that it had been their pleasure, and he hoped they would all enjoy the pleasure-grounds, making sure not to miss the palm house and the grotto, which, he assured the guests, were rather special. Curate Palmer then took the opportunity to announce that the standard of the choir had reached the level at which it could join the massed Temperance Choir at the concert in the Crystal Palace. This was received with gasps of pleasure and amazement by all those in the garden. Of course, this performance would also involve a trip to London by train, something that was really special.

'Now enjoy the flowers,' he concluded, so Alice and Florence took him at his word and walked to the nearest flower beds, chatting excitedly over this latest news.

Unfortunately, two of the boy trebles from St Mary's church choir followed closely behind them.

'Too hot for you Indians?' shouted one.

'You forgot yor elifunts,' called the other.

'Pretend they're not there,' Alice said to Florence, and they quickened their pace until – *click* – a small stone landed by their feet making them skip a little.

'*Stop that*, you boys!' A loud voice shouted from behind them. '*Clear off!*'

When the sisters turned around, they saw two young men, tenors from the choir, waving the small hooligans away. Richard and Peter were choristers from St Marys.

Alice had previously noticed Richard's voice during choir practice and recognised him from the tone of his shout.

'Those little devils ought to know how to behave when they see pretty young ladies,' he continued.

'Let's show you some more of the gardens without your being bothered anymore,' said the other young man, Peter. So, with a smile and a nod, the sisters continued their walk, but this time Alice walked by the side of Richard, and Florence walked with Peter as the young men reeled off the names of the flowers.

'Would you like to see the grotto? It really is something rather splendid,' said Richard, pointing to a small hill at the far end of the garden.

'The entrance is on the far side and it is a bit dark in there.'

'Dear me,' said Florence, 'I think I would be quite scared in a dark cave.'

'I'll stay with you outside while the other two go in,' said Peter, pointing to a wooden seat nearby. 'Off you go, you two.'

'The waterfall inside makes all of the paving a bit slippery, so you'd better give me your hand,' Richard told Alice, and so they descended the few steps together.

The gardeners had put a small lamp inside the grotto in order to make all of the sea creatures traced in seashells glow a little.

'They show better with some light,' Richard continued. 'If you look at the ceiling you can see that those shells are set in the pattern of the sky.'

Alice looked upwards and marvelled at the stars.

Richard pointed, 'Look, there's Orion with his belt.'

'Oohh yes.'

'And over there's the planet Venus.'

'Where?'

'You're not looking in the right direction. Look…' And he lifted his fingers to touch Alice's neck, then ran them upwards until he tilted her head towards a bright star.

'There, d'you see.' He touched her cheek.

'Yes, oohh yes.'

Alice lowered her head and in the dim light her eyes shone. She also caught the shine in Richard's, now close to hers, and as she lowered her head he kissed her gently on her lips.

'My beautiful star,' he said softly.

Peter called from outside. 'Come along, or the ice cream will have all melted.'

Blinking, they climbed up the wet steps and joined the other two, hands touching.

'I'll have to sponge that green patch from the back of your dress before we get home,' Florence told her sister.

Talk at the dinner table that evening was animated, reflecting the exciting time Florence and Alice had spent at the 'big' house. Their mother wanted to know everything, and she was so pleased that the new dresses had been such a success.

'And what were the strawberries like?' She wanted to know. 'Were they huge and did they have thick cream? And was the garden very pretty? And,' a slight pause, 'did every one behave?'

'There were some nasty little boys who threw stones at us,' Florence told her.

'But Peter and Richard chased them off,' added her sister.

'Peter and Richard?'

'Yes, you know, two tenors from St Mary's choir. They found the ice cream for us. It was delicious.'

Their mother's brow returned to its normal position but she gave Bertram a knowing look. They knew that the young men were singers from St Marys and, too, that they were the sons of tradesmen in the town.

She smiled at her daughters, 'I'm sure Miss McGregor kept her eye on things.'

And the conversation moved back to the dresses and a possible visit to the Crystal Palace later in the month with the Temperance Choir.

Chapter 6

CRYSTAL PALACE

The next time they had dinner together, the girls told their parents that a special anthem had been written for the Temperance Movement which had to be learned perfectly.

'And we're all going up to London to sing it as a massed choir.'

The Reverend Palmer had organised free transport – to be offered by the local Great Western Railway director – and had also organised a supply of buns and lemonade for the journey from the Temperance café, paid for by subscriptions from supportive diners.

Everyone was in a good mood during the trip up to London where they joined several other choirs from other parts of the country. The Reverend Palmer was not surprised to see several choirs from the North, where he knew the Temperance movement was strongly favoured. The anthem went well, with the combined effect of almost one thousand voices being overwhelming, especially with the added booming background of the huge organ.

'I could feel the vibrations going right through my body,' Florence told her sister after the singing finished.

'Me too,' Alice responded.

The excitement carried over on to the train journey home when the two St Mary's tenors, Richard and Peter, arrived with some left-over buns and offered to share them with the girls. The two couples sat closely together on the bench seat of the railway carriage all the way back, with the girls sitting together in the middle and each boy sitting next to his favourite. The ever-watchful Miss McGregor, recognising the sparkle in the eyes of her young ladies, insisted on seeing the girls safely home from the station when they arrived back.

Bertram and Emma were pleased with the way in which their daughters had mixed-in with the other singers and were on the whole delighted with how quickly the family had settled into town ways and with the townspeople.

Bertram thought that the Church would be very pleased with the progress he had made in his new position, especially as Church attendance numbers were growing. He liked to think that some of this new popularity was due to the freshness of the editorial style he had brought to his newspaper, and he started to compose an article along the lines of *Township and Fellowship* for the next edition. He was careful not to give too much credit to the Reverend Palmer in the process, since at heart he regarded the other as a rival for the town's souls, but he did highlight the mix of creeds and beliefs that went to make up the impressive sound of those massed voices.

'Something of which the town can be proud,' he concluded; and repeated the point in his next sermon.

Chapter 7

EELS

While the Moorehouse sisters' school closed for a short holiday for part of the summer – as Miss McGregor took her usual visit to Scotland to visit her family – the shops in the town were even busier during these summer months. Members of the Council nodded wisely at this development, telling themselves that the increased business was all of their doing, yet their smugness was not without some justification. Some of the increased trade coming to the town was the result of having a good railway connection, but the Council itself had taken several steps to make the place more attractive to visitors. Keeping the streets clean and litter-free was a start, but the removal of the cluttered open market in the central square, with its 'Shambles' of food stalls and meat preparation and all of the associated smells and odours, was the most noticeable improvement. This allowed a fine sight of the new Town Hall as the centrepiece which could be admired as visitors crossed the bridge and entered the town.

Councillors gave themselves most credit for the

establishment of the rowing regatta, which was the main feature of the summer season. The course ran from the remodelled bridge upstream as far as the island, on which the owner had given permission to the lodge of the wealthier Masons to build a small Greek-style temple for their meetings. The Council had then done its part by straightening the course through the removal of part of the bank on the flood side of the river. This created a stretch of water wide and straight enough to allow two rowing eights to race each other side by side. This rowing advantage was quickly spotted by Oxford and Cambridge Universities who arranged to stage their annual regatta there. The spectators enjoyed splendid scenery along the riverbanks for their picnics and the funfairs and entertainments that soon appeared in the surrounding meadows. These same spectators then continued their celebrations in the hotels and pubs throughout the town for as long as these establishments stayed open.

Local tradesmen quickly seized on these advantages and made the most of them. The majority of these tradespeople were Councillors themselves, who then promoted the other advantages of the town as a resort with good facilities for boating, fishing, painting, and swimming. Opposite the main boat-hire business was a stretch of greensward divided into two and backed with that series of changing huts which Bertram had observed from the bridge on his first visit. This was the new swimming lido for men and women and was a major attraction on hot summer days. Some visitors were tempted to stay longer in the town and a new hotel was planned opposite the railway station while several of the larger houses started to offer overnight lodging with breakfasts.

It was on a pleasant summer morning that Emma decided to stroll through the main area of the town at its decorated best, with each arm of the crossroads in the middle of the town hung with bunting and flags. Ladies had already bought dresses for the festivities and the Emporium was quiet, but Emma paused to admire the window display which had been specially created by a senior saleslady. Mr. Chapman himself was engaged with the supervision of council affairs and such tourists as came by train quickly gravitated towards the river. Later, during her mid-day break, Emma decided to look at the upper and quieter end of the town. As she strolled, she noticed the butcher's shop of Hyatt and Son, 'Suppliers of Fresh Meat, Sausages and Pies to the Gentry.' A young man, about twenty years old, was vigorously sweeping the pavement with a bass broom. He looked up when he saw that he was obstructing her way. 'I'm very sorry to hinder you, Madam, but we have just killed a pig and we have to wash away the blood as soon as we can down this drain outside the shop. So, if you will excuse me I'll soon make your path nice and clean again.'

But just as he started scrubbing, he stopped and looked up at her.

'Aren't you Mrs Moorehouse, the mother of the two new girls in the Choir? I'm one of St Mary's tenors and I think I know them. I saw small boys throwing stones at them – and my friend and I put a stop to such nonsense. Perhaps they may have mentioned this to you?' Then, a little embarrassed, he went on, 'We also went to the Temperance event at the Crystal Palace on the same train and shared some of the buns.'

'Oh yes, you must be Peter.' Then Emma corrected herself. 'No, Richard, isn't it?'

'Yes, my name is Richard Hyatt. I hope that they've recovered from their stoning.'

'Oh, yes, thank you, I'll tell them you enquired after them.'

A short pause followed because neither knew what to say and Emma started to move away. Richard put up his hand to stop her. 'I wondered, Mrs Moorehouse…if I could ask your permission…to visit your girls, along with my friend…? No…what I mean is, could I take them out one day? You see, what I have in mind is to see if they would like to come with me tomorrow when I have our donkey, and I'm going to walk upstream to the next weir to collect some eels for my father. This is his shop.' He pointed to the door behind him. 'He sells eels from a tank.' He stumbled on. 'I could show them a swan's nest with five baby swans. I'm sure that they would like that.'

Emma, for whom all this was sudden and new, regained her self-composure.

'Why don't you come to the manse tomorrow morning and ask them yourself?'

At nine o'clock the following morning, Richard appeared at the front door of the manse accompanied by the butcher's delivery donkey, Sally. Mrs. Dorkins indicated that the tradesmen's entrance was at the rear of the building, but Richard quickly explained that it was the suggestion of Mrs. Moorehouse that had given him the courage to call, to ask if the girls would fancy a trip to the upstream lock on the donkey. He explained his father had arranged the collection of eels caught by the water bailiff of the estate and he was to bring them back to the shop.

'It's a lovely day,' he added, 'and it's a pleasant walk along the river upstream to the next lock. The girls could share a ride on the donkey there but they'd have to walk back.

'Please, please go and ask the girls.'

Mrs. Dorkins returned to say that Alice would like to see the swan's nest and would be down in a minute, but

Florence was rather poorly today and would rather not come. The mention of the nest told Richard that their mother had given her approval. After a short while, Alice appeared in her light summer dress and Richard moved a pannier to one side so that she could sit side-saddle on the donkey.

They were soon out of the town and away from the houses. Richard chatted away, pointing out all of the new summer flowers, often by name. From her lofty seat Alice was able to appreciate the flow of greenish warm water with, now and then, a splash as a fish snapped a fly. She pointed out the multi-coloured dragonflies, and, 'Over there!' a hare leaping from their approach.

'Did he have his ears up?'

'Yes, I told you he did.'

'That really was a hare then,' Richard confirmed. 'The other morning a friend of mine was walking downstream on the other side of the river and in five miles he counted sixty hares playing in the meadows. If he shoots one or two he brings them into dad's shop for us to sell, and they don't hang around. They're so good.'

Then, 'Look, just in the water, five baby swans. I said we'd see them. Watch out for the cob, these males can be vicious if they think you're too near to their young.'

Alice was transported by the slow-moving beauty of the experience and was briefly reminded of the brownish muddy bank of the river near to her earlier childhood home. But soon she was brought back to the present as the reedy banks gave way to lush meadows and she saw the herd of cows belonging to the manor grazing near their farm.

'Nearly there.' Richard interrupted her thoughts.

'Hello there, over here!' The loud voice of Douglas, the water bailiff, directed them to a small inlet a little way below the weir, the rushing of which they could hear a little way off. He was accompanied by two small girls, each about ten years old.

'These are me'lord's daughters, Stephanie and Pauline, sent over to help.' Both girls gave a smile and a small wave.

'Bin here before and they've to gather the horse radish for the sauce. This is for the guest table at the Hall, to go with the eels,' he added by way of explanation.

'Come on you lot, let's get started.' Douglas led the way to the inlet and climbed into a small boat which he pushed off until he reached a rope hanging from a low tree branch. Then he hauled the rope until a large black mass emerged on the end, which he swung into the boat.

'It's moving!' Alice squealed and held Richard's hand tighter.

'Of course it is, they're the live eels we came for.'

Douglas called up from the boat, 'Ow many your father want?'

'About a guinea's 'orth.'

It was only then that Alice realised that the whole wriggling mass consisted of eels firmly attached with their mouths to a horse's head, which had a rope through the sockets where the horse's eyes had been. No one noticed her look of horror as they watched Douglas counting forty eels into the sack that Robert took from the saddle bag on Sally.

'A couple extra for the Reverend for his table.' Douglas thrust some more eels into the sack before wiping his hands on his apron.

'And you'll need some horse radish to go with them.' Stephanie pushed in a couple of roots they had just dug from the bank behind them.

'Oh, thank you. Father will be pleased.'

The two little girls wore no shoes and were quite muddy from the efforts of digging the horseradish, looking not at all like the daughters of the Lord of the Manor, but they gave a happy laugh as Alice gave each a small kiss of thanks.

Richard stood aloof. 'Catholics!' he whispered behind his hand to Alice. 'No money there.'

After crossing the meadow on their return, the little party entered a shady group of alder trees where Sally stopped in a patch of shade.

'This is her favourite spot for lunch, she'll not move on until she has had her fill of that soft green grass over there. Let's sit on the bank of the river until she's ready to move on. We can dabble our toes in the water.'

'Oh, yes.' But after a minute or two, his accomplice turned her head around and fixed her eyes on a wild briar.

'Look at those dog roses at the top in the sun. Perhaps you could reach a few to take home to my mother. She would be pleased.'

Richard leapt up and made his way to the flowers, but when he returned his companion had disappeared, leaving a pile of clothes in her place.

'Come on in,' called a voice from the river and Richard saw the white form of his friend with her head just above the water, waving to him.

'Don't go too far in, the current's very strong in the middle. I'll come and help you.'

He stripped off his clothes to his undershorts and waded into the cool greenish water as it flowed past. Much splashing and teasing took place before they emerged together and then lay down to dry off in the hot sun. Children's bath memories seemed to overcome their earlier embarrassment and they became dry as they waited for their clothes to dry in the sun and for Sally to finish grazing.

Richard had one more task to perform however.

'Saw 'em in the reeds when we were in the water.' He

rolled up his trouser legs and paddled up to the reed bed. After bending down with his hands submerged, he stood up and threw large black pebbles on to the grassy bank, only stopping when there were about six, each of them of about six or so inches long.

'Swan mussels,' he explained. 'My dad loves 'em. Say's they're better than oysters when he can get them. He'll be pleased with these.'

'What a lovely day,' Alice beamed as they made their way home, walking on either side of the donkey. Even Sally seemed to smile when Richard placed a rose in her mane; the bag of eels wriggled in their dark sack as it warmed during the journey on her back. At home, Alice's mother was delighted with her roses; Mrs. Dorkins less so with the eels, but she managed to jelly them for the family the next day. Florence said that they were 'horrible.'

The summer passed with walks along the river banks, sometimes with sister Florence and Peter, sometimes not, usually after the morning services when the foursome would meet at the bridge. They never tired of the intoxication of lush meadows, with the background of distant rounded green hills, and always with the rich smell of the warm river and the changing season's offerings of wild flowers. All of these experiences created luscious memories that filled this summer season of the two young immigrants from India.

Chapter 8

THE REGATTA

As the summer blossomed, so did the little town; with
several marriages, flower shows, school prize-giving events,
and many other celebrations that were just waiting for the
fine weather. All of these occasions required a comment or
two in the local papers and Bertram found that he was more
and more involved in recording these principal occasions,
especially those involving Methodist churchgoers, and he
needed to spend more time working on the editorial side
of the *Advertiser*. In particular he found that on Thursdays
and Fridays his time was needed to get the layout ready for
printing. He shared his worries with Mr. Clegg, the church
caretaker, and he suggested that the morning service be
dropped at those busy times. Later, Bertram informed his
faithful congregation of his decision to close the church in
the mornings during regatta week. Nobody spoke against
this suggestion, which was in line with the actions of most
of the congregation for that week, and Clegg approved of
it. All of the able town residents made their way with their

picnics to the river banks to watch the racing which now occupied the full six days. St Mary's church, which had the historically important position at the town end of the bridge, always arranged a special regatta service to start the events on the Sunday before the racing started. This took a large proportion of Bertram's population away, so anyway he did not feel that he had abandoned his flock. The excuse he gave to those who asked, and really only Clegg questioned him, was that he had been invited as editor to travel behind the umpire's launch in order to obtain the correct race results for his paper. Bertram did not mention to Clegg that in fact the invitation to join the launch had been given by Chapman to Emma.

On the Tuesday of the previous week the Emporium owner had entered his premises in some excitement and immediately took Emma from her usual chair at the front of the shop, quietly whispering in her ear.

'We've just been offered the use of one of Hedge's slipper launches for a day during the regatta and it was agreed that I, as Emporium owner, should use it for the day, wearing my Alderman's chain of office to confirm the strong links that the town has with the regatta committee. I'm sure you've noticed these beautiful craft gliding through the water without a sound. The new boats are powered by the new electric batteries.'

He explained to her that they got charged at Hedges Boatyard every evening and then can go a whole day on the river with no further attention.

Here Chapman took a few breaths to recover and continued, 'Well I thought you might like to accompany me on the town launch for the day as a token of my thanks for your handling my business while I'm away.'

A pause, and then he added, as though it had only just

come to mind, 'Of course, Bertram is invited too. It will be good for the Church for him to be seen and it will be some thanks for all of his efforts with the paper.' He cleared his throat, 'Perhaps he could write a nice report of the day,' he added as an afterthought. '"The Emporium; town's major supporter of the regatta", something along those lines.'

The beautiful summer riverside proved to be the perfect background for Emma to show off one of their light Indian dresses, and she told her daughters that they might join their friends for the day if they wished. No second push was needed since it had already been suggested that the foursome walk upstream to the sanctuary where the river swans had been ushered to prevent any damage to them during the rowing. The last thing the town wanted was trouble with the Swan Uppers following any damage to the property of the Queen.

As the crowds arrived by the special trains put on by the GWR for the first day of the annual event, Bertram and Emma dressed in their best light summer Indian clothes, and made their way through the town to the quayside. They were met by Chapman wearing his best white suit as requested by Hedges, standing on the rear deck of the shiny electric launch which had been bedecked with bunting ready for a day's racing.

During the racing, their craft followed the umpire's vessel up and down the course as each race took place. Wicker chairs had been provided for them and Emma waved to all of her friends, to customers, employees, and anyone else who acknowledged their prime floating position. Bertram nodded to those church attendees he recognised and now and then he nudged Emma if he thought she was over-reacting to the glory of the occasion. Inwardly he glowed with the realisation that this was really the symbol of their being accepted into town society. A splendid lunch was given at the Stewards' Enclosure and this was followed by a further programme of racing in the afternoon.

'This is good old England at its best,' mused Bertram later that afternoon as he was gently rocked by the water. 'It is why I came home,' he told his inner self. 'And why would not the Church be pleased with this role I've taken on?'

Throughout the summer there was an increasingly large number of invitations to church and school fêtes, garden parties, and other fund-raising occasions, which filled their season. Their fine looks and elegant bearing made Emma and her daughters welcome guests at many of the town social events, but the girls' close friends, Richard and Peter, were often working – and in any case were not invited to such events. The two young men nevertheless managed to join the girls on Sunday afternoons when the four walked along one or other of the river banks with the Temperance Sunday Society, which was led by several single ladies from the town church.. Tea was taken at one of the river lock cafés before returning after the pleasant afternoon stroll. This public event was approved of by the girls' parents and was a welcome taste of freedom for the two sisters, who never mentioned the depressions in the long meadow grass where they lay on the coats of their young men, hidden from the main walking group, and where they planned their futures.

Richard was sure that he would take over the family butcher's shop, which was very successful as the main supplier in the town now that the market traders had been forbidden to kill and sell fresh products from market stalls. Mr. Hyatt, Richard's father, was the beneficiary of this ruling. His business had hugely increased. Richard was less pleased, as the burden of running of the daily workload in the shop had fallen on his shoulders.

'Not for much longer,' he told his friends. 'Soon we'll be selling fish, and probably cooked meats starting with ham. We may even be opening a separate fish shop.' This fancy was stopped as his mouth was closed by a kiss from Alice.

'What about you, Peter?' Florence asked him. 'What do you want to do?'

'Well, I'm not going to be a hairdresser like my father. For a start, the business isn't big enough. My uncle's going to work for the new people coming to town. Have you heard of Timothy Whites? They sell bottled medicines and hardware, cups and saucers, and all of that sort of thing. Well, he wants me to help him on the chemist's side but it'll mean training to be a proper pharmaceutical chemist. It'll mean doing lessons at home and on Wednesdays I'll have to go to London for lectures.'

'How exciting,' Florence told him. And they continued their dreams in the grass.

Chapter 9

THE CRICKET MATCH

The main social event at the end of the summer was the final cricket match of the season, taken very seriously by Bertram who had been informed that it was expected his whole family would attend. Everyone else would be there in their best summer outfits and the occasion would give the new Methodist minister a chance to show his family to the inhabitants of the town and really demonstrate that they had been accepted and were now part of town society. Around the cricket ground today, there were picnic groups consisting of family members of the players, and some visitors from out of town who had stabled their horses at the livery company. There were even some groups of visitors who had arrived by the new train service. The ladies' group from the Methodist Chapel sold cold lemon barley water made with fresh water drawn from the new artesian well in the brewery yard, the temperature of which was much appreciated as it was several degrees below the heated air of the cricket ground. Emma helped these ladies pour the drinks and the rest of the family sat in their new canvas chairs while Bertram wrote notes on the details of the game for his newspaper. This was the first time the family had enjoyed such a town event together and the atmosphere seemed very pleasant. He recognised several members of his congregation who spoke a few words to him as they took their positions around the boundary to enjoy a good view of the game, along with their afternoon picnic tea. Bertram nodded to Mr. Clegg who had removed the jacket of his work-a-day suit, sitting in the shade next to the cricket pavilion in his position as scorer. Mr. Clegg waved his pencil in acknowledgment of the greeting.

The town's premier cricket ground was a piece of a grassy field behind the headquarters of the local rowing club, and this had been given such extensive treatment by the cricket club groundsman that it truly deserved the term 'hallowed'. The family were comfortably ensconced in their chairs and Mrs. Dorkins had packed a fine picnic of cucumber sandwiches and fairy cakes, accompanied by a large flagon of Temperance lemon barley water brought over by Emma. Bertram tried to explain a little of the rules of the game so that his ladies understood why the men carrying wooden bats became either 'in' or 'out,' and Emma and her daughters pretended not to understand, although they'd often enjoyed a similar lecture in India, where the game was also very popular.

'Why is one team wearing white trousers and the other wearing grey trousers?' Alice teased her father, knowing full well he would struggle to explain this anomaly.

'Well you see, the white trousered players are all members of the town team and play here all the time. They're mainly the sons of tradesmen in the town, most of them Freemasons. The others in the grey trousers are apprentices and working lads from the Mechanics Institute who were working all of this morning and have come straight here from work. They usually play on a piece of meadow just past the railway station, so this is a very important game for them. It is played once a year to see who the best fellows are. So they use the best ground...you see.'

This explanation made no sense to Alice and Florence, but Emma nodded her head in order to deflect her husband to the picnic, which needed a man to distribute plates of good food without getting jam on summer frocks.

Bertram felt extremely pleased to have been invited by the Mayor, Mr. Brandish senior, to attend this important town event and he told himself that now he was really being accepted by all those in the town who mattered. Brandish explained that the churches were all represented there, with the vicar of St Mary's being one of the umpires and the curate of All Saints being the other. He asked if Bertram could attend the traditional dinner which followed the match at the Assembly Rooms to say Grace for them. Bertram said he would be delighted and explained that his family loved a game of cricket and would be present at the ground.

Professionally, as editor of an important newspaper, he took notes for his readers, who were certainly waiting to read the result of the match.

The curate from All Saints standing as umpire wore a long white coat and was immobile, humming a few hymn tunes to himself as he waited for Sunday to come around. The game proceeded at a slow pace in the warm sunshine and one or two of the spectators closed their eyes.

The soft meadow turf absorbed the heavy tread of the large, cream-trousered player as he accelerated towards the stumps and hurled the red missile towards the other end, where a grey-trousered apprentice flailed his willow bat through the warm summer air. The ball thudded into the gloves of the wicket keeper who threw it into the air with a loud appeal, '*Owzaat!*'

The match had reached a keenly-balanced stage where the two teams had scored an almost equal number of runs and the afternoon was drawing to a close.

'Howzat!,' yelled Rupert Brandish, a white-trousered player, pointedly tonguing the 't' and placing his perspiring red face within inches of that of the Reverend Palmer, so as to make fierce eye contact.

The Palmer head, now under a pile of players' sun hats, moved from left to right and as it moved, indicated that no contact had been made by the ball as it passed the bat.

'Not out,' said all of his senses. But his eyes read the contrary in signs visible everywhere else.

'Out,' said the large letters on the roof of the tea tent.

'Out,' said the wet towel covering the large barrel of Harvest Ale.

'Out,' said the huge letters running down the chimney of the brewery on the other side of the river, spelling the surname of the angry bowler.

A cloud of the aromatic vapour of brewing hops then came across the river into the nostrils of the vicar of St Marys, the town church which stood adjacent to the brewery, who was officiating as square leg umpire and who now went over to his colleague, Palmer.

'I thought I heard a snick,' he simpered.

Curate Palmer raised his finger and aligned it with the chimney over the river.

'Out!' came the murmur.

The grey-trousered youth then spat on the pitch as he removed his gloves before making for the barrel of Harvest Ale in the shady tent for his free refreshment provided by the Brandish Company. A hiss of incredulity came from the parasols and sunshades around the ground. This natural antagonism towards the umpires was expected from spectators who witnessed this blatant bending of the rules, since this sequence of events followed a pattern which was similar every year. The apprentices expected to lose, the goodwill sponsorship of their Christmas celebration by the Brandish establishment depended on it.

One man in particular, though, did not want to lose. William Climand, the twenty-year-old son of George Climand, the builder. It was said that William was born with a silver trowel in one hand and a brick in the other and was a chip off his father's block. He lived in his father's new mansion built on a hill above the town from the discarded masonry of the Old Town Hall. Now at the crease, he faced the Brandish fast bowler. *Swish*, the first ball was sent over the boundary for six. *Chop*, the second was guided to the other end of the ground. Four more. Cheers!! Next ball sent skywards and was lost for a few minutes in the grass outside of the ground, another six. Then William smashed the final ball over the boundary near the beer tent, a further six. Twenty clouted runs, enough to win. The apprentices poured on to the pitch and carried their hero towards the free Harvest Special ale. Christmas sponsorship could wait while the winners relished the moment.

Later the report in the *Standard* read, 'Rupert Brandish gave a fine performance in his role as principal fast bowler for the town cricket team on Saturday when the Town beat the Apprentices handsomely. This result arose when the umpires disallowed the score of an Apprentice player who was considered as no longer living in the town and who was therefore not eligible to play.'

No one was at all surprised by this report. After all,

William lived with his mother and father in their new house constructed from the dismantled Old Town Hall – in the adjacent county. The moral victory was, though, claimed by the 'grey trousers' who held the high ground.

'Take the girls home without me,' Bertram told Emma after the match ended. 'The boys have asked me to say Grace before tonight's dinner at the Assembly Rooms. This is their end of season celebration, you know. I won't be late,' and he kissed her on the cheek.

But it was past midnight when she heard the knocking on the front door and as she opened it, recoiled, appalled at the sight of the blood-covered face of her husband.

'The Rev walked into a lamppost on his way home and needed a bit of an 'and,' the constable who was supporting Bertram on the steps to his front door, told her. 'I fink he's broke 'is nose.'

'How on earth did this happen to you? Who saw you fall over?' Emma assailed her husband when she had dragged him in and closed the door. She had been waiting all evening, imagining all of the worst possibilities, but never including that her abstemious husband would be delivered home by the police. Drunk!

'No one saw us, it wash dark.' Bertram stammered, adding, 'Only that nice poleeshman who knew where I lived. It wash dark,' he repeated.

'It was not dark all evening. Some of the players at the cricket dinner must have seen you drinking all that beer.'

'It washn't beer,' he hiccuped. 'It was lemonade… shandy topped with Harvest Shpecial. It wash bloody hot in that sun today an evr'y one sweated like pigs, 'cludin me in m' black suit.' Another pause. 'They ran out of lemonade so old Cleggsy topped me glass up with Harvest Shpecial. A few times, I think. "To help the singing", he said.'

'Singing!' Emma gave up and tried to recover some of the lost dignity.

'I hope you have written your sermon for tomorrow, because it's too late now. You were only supposed to say Grace for them, not join in the party.'

'Well, I only got them singing *Onward Chrishtian Soljers*...sheveral times. Which was better than in Church.'

'Oh dear. What're you going to do tomorrow?'

'I shall jusht shay I'm feeling a bit poorly and would you mind if I give the shermon while I am shitting. I mean shitting down.'

'Oh, my Lord,' breathed Emma to herself. 'This is supposed to be a Temperance Chapel.'

She tried to clean her husband's suit and the next morning Mrs. Dorkins tried to remove the bloodstains from his shirt, but Bertram performed the four sacred services in his reduced state, his face much swollen, with a sticky bandage on his nose, in clothes that were still damp – and slightly pink. Prayers and responses came out with much stammering and hesitation, the sermon shortened to the minimum permissible length.

No one said anything to him at the door as they left, not even Mr. Chapman, but looks and whispers told it all.

'Not that old elephant stuff again,' was one whisper that was loud enough for Bertram to hear, even in his hungover state.

'Oh dear, oh dear, oh dear!' went through his brain all day long. 'What damage I have done! What about Emma and the girls? What a disgrace!'

The policeman had been told by his superiors not to mention this incident, which was not considered serious in a town with sixty public houses for a population of five thousand. Simple drunkenness was acceptable so long as there was no fighting with injuries – even domestic violence towards wives or partners was ignored. Seeing a gentleman back to his home at night after a celebration was considered part of a constable's regular duty, which need not be recorded. That is to say, 'Not mentioned officially.' In fact, Bertram's little adventure was the subject of whispered comment by everyone in the town during the next two weeks, even though the editor of the rival paper also chose to view Bertram's 'accident' as a non-news item. One anonymous churchgoer however thought it serious enough to inform Methodist Headquarters in London.

After dinner conversation on Sunday at the manse table was subdued for a while and an attempt by Bertram to liven up things by singing a verse or two of the 'funny' songs he had learnt at the cricket dinner were treated with silence by his family, although Mrs. Dorkins had a little smile to herself in the kitchen. Everyone knew everything about his fall from grace, but friends and townsfolk treated the family ladies only with silent smiles of sympathy. But the Church knew.

Chapter 10

CONTRITION

Three gentlemen in black suits descended from the 'Flyer' as it pulled in to the station two weeks later and they walked quickly through the town directly to the vestry of the Methodist Church. Mr. Chapman, the two senior ladies, and Mr. Clegg were waiting, seated on the hard chairs along one long side of the business table. The three visitors joined the town group, with the Reverend Grimes in the centre, flanked by two note-takers. A single hard chair was placed on the opposite side of the table.

'Have you told him we were coming?' the senior visitor asked Mr. Clegg. The Reverend Grimes received a confirmatory nod, then continued.

'Very well then, we may begin. Please call the Reverend Moorehouse in, Mr. Clegg, and let us get this nasty business started.'

Mr. Clegg did as he was told, and Bertram sat in the vacant chair.

'Now, Moorehouse, the Church has received some

very disturbing news concerning your behaviour here in the town. News of the ways in which you have carried out your duties as a leader of the Methodist community; news of your behaviour towards the Temperance Movement; and of your abandonment of our spiritual ideals for personal gain. All this results in a considerable lack of leadership on your part in a growing community which looks to the Methodist church for spiritual and behavioural guidance.'

Bertram, who was just expecting a stern warning for his performance in church the Sunday following the cricket match, for which he was ready to claim temporary illness, was taken aback by this longer tirade.

'But…but…' he stuttered, 'I…I…do not understand what you are saying. What have I done that was wrong?'

'Your inebriated behaviour at the cricket dinner, when you led the singing of anti-temperance songs while standing on a table, was the final straw.'

'I only drank lemonade, and after the Grace I only encouraged the singing of *Onward Christian Soldiers*. Everyone joined in and I thought the hymn quite appropriate.'

The inquisition leader thundered, 'You continued to add Harvest Ale to your glass, and then led the singing of *The Flies Crawled up the Window*. Did you not know that this has anti-temperance words in the verse where "five thousand flies crawled up the window, but it was the Crystal Palace, and they were never seen again"? This is a clear anti-Temperance sentiment and you led the singing! You made us the laughing stock of the town. On the following day, Sunday, in Church you made several references to Buddhism and its compassionate attitude towards elephants. Sunday is a *Christian* day, or have you forgotten? Our Lord was not a Buddhist!'

Bertram's memory of all of this was blurred, so he just hung his head.

'These lapses of behaviour get carried into your *Advertiser* where you refuse to condemn the excessive drunkenness in this area, and you even give prominence to the advertising of alcoholic beverages.'

At last the worm turned. 'No, that is wrong and unfair, I would never do such a thing.'

'Are you not aware that 'Butler's Health Tonic' is based on full-strength sherry and that there are several addicts to it in the town? And that it is advertised prominently on your front page?'

The two lady members of the committee nodded their heads in knowing approval at this revelation, hinting at where this information originated.

Grimes was apoplectic with rage and his face was bright red. 'But worst of all, you stopped morning services during regatta week, you heathen!'

'Do you think, Moorehouse, the church is just somewhere to shelter from the rain during regatta week?' A few seconds went by as Grimes's natural pink shade returned to his face. He took a sip of water before delivering sentence, as it were.

'The Church takes all of this dereliction of your position extremely seriously and you will hear further of these matters. For the moment we advise, nay demand that you dispose of your interests in the *Advertiser*, which you obviously treat as your main source of income, and immediately cease publishing it. I suggest in future you treat your flock with Christian concern and humility.'

Grimes glared at the miserable figure of Bertram. 'You are dismissed!'

Bertram stood and left the room without a word. The

two clerks closed their notebooks.

Bertram did not come home for dinner that evening. Emma was worried because she had no idea where her husband had disappeared to. Her thoughts wandered towards the river but she quickly dismissed this nightmare. Bertie was much too sensible, and self-centred, she thought. Nothing as drastic as that.

Acting on this hunch Emma walked down to the river and found her husband in the middle of the bridge looking at the slowly-moving dark green water. His eyes were moist as he studied the remaining waterfowl as they made their way to their nests. He tried to reconcile his warm feelings towards his friends in the town and compared the kind gestures of welcome he had received with the harshness of the treatment doled out to him by the committee.

Emma heard him mutter, 'Life is mirrored by this flow of the river and The Lord will be bringing other good things which will heal the hurt I have just received.' She took his hand in hers and led him back to their home. Neither spoke.

Chapter 11

Confessions!

The following morning Mrs. Dorkins informed Emma that her husband had already left on the morning milk train at five o'clock. Bertie had not mentioned anything of his future plans and Emma was worried by this strange turn of events. Finally, she took the girls to school, which was to be the last one for Alice now she was eighteen. She kissed them goodbye on their cheeks, and started her wander through the main street of the town until she reached Chapman's Emporium and Haberdashers, where she made her way to her usual chair. Business was quiet.

A word was passed down to her that Chapman wished to see her as soon as she arrived. Something important then.

'Good morning, Mrs. Moorehouse, thank you for coming up so quickly. Please shut the door, I have something very confidential to discuss with you.' Mr. Chapman seemed all in a rush to get started. Before she could turn back to the door, he brushed past her.

'Please sit.' He hurried to shut the door himself and offered her a chair.

'If it's about Bertie, I'm sure he is very sorry about what has happened and it will never happen again.' At least not while he is married to me, she thought to herself.

'No, no. Nothing about that. I am sure the Church will forgive, just as Jesus forgave. If we cannot forgive, what are we? It lifts us above the animals,' he grandly misquoted. 'No, no, something much more serious than that.'

In the circumstances, Emma was surprised. 'Really?' And waited for the next announcement.

'The Mayor, Dr. Redesdale, has disappeared, left the town with his supply of laudanum that he had collected from his poppy garden, and his instruments, and money. He has not paid any of his bills and no one knows where he is. The Council thinks he has gone for good, skipped abroad you know, probably back to Calcutta where he came from. So the town needs a new Mayor quickly. It really is my turn for the job but I have always said the business here keeps me too busy. But most of the other Aldermen are Freemasons and are in brewing – or related affairs – hotels and public houses, y'know.' And Chapman took a few deep breaths.

'They want me to take over now until the end of the current term.'

This solution to the problem had only been arrived at after much discussion at the Masonic Lodge, and afterwards in the Red Lion.

'Dear Mrs. Moorehouse, I do not have the time to run the town *and* the Emporium. What shall I do if I have to leave the business to run itself?' Mr. Chapman sounded a little panicky.

Emma stood, walked over to Chapman, and patted

him on the back as she had done many times in the past to her daughters.

'There, there, you are taking this this honour too seriously. Look, I will come here each morning and watch over things for you. Your cashier will take care of all of the money and bank affairs and I will take care of all of the rest. You can spend all of your day looking splendid in your robes and chain, telling the Town Clerk how to run the Town.'

'That would be possible, of course but,' he sighed, 'they say I must become a Freemason. There, I've said it.'

'So be it, Mr. Chapman, if that is what they want, but as they know you are a Temperance stalwart, say you will be a non-alcoholic Freemason.'

Mr. Chapman began to look less harassed. He stood and looked out of the window, sticking his thumbs in his braces.

'Yes, that's right. A Temperance Mayor and Freemason. That will be good for the town for once. As he sat down he stepped over to Emma and gave her a hug but recoiled quickly when he realised he may have pushed the bounds of propriety a little far.

'Thank you my dear. Thank you very much.'

A gleam started in the corner of Emma's eye; it was followed by a smile.

'Why don't you make it a condition of your acceptance that as a sign of bringing the town together, the Masons must merge their *Standard* with the Temperance *Advertiser*. It will then be the true symbol of a united town.'

After a few moments thought, Chapman beamed.

'That is a wonderful idea. Do you think it will work? Will Bertie let go of his pet hobby'?

'He will if I suggest it to him and show that he'll be able to spend more time with his flock.'

Chapman sounded relieved. 'Well then, let us get things moving straight away.'

Later in the day, the Town Clerk-cum-Masonic Lodge Scribe was told to obtain funds to fix the merger of the two journals.

'I will see you here tomorrow morning then, dear Mrs. Moorehouse, and I will make this official in the meantime with a proper agreement between us with a proper wage for you. No! No! No arguments please.' Chapman leaned towards Emma to shake her hand, then, as an afterthought, bent a bit further and kissed her cheek. 'Thank you my dear. Thank you very much.'

Thus, in the absence of her husband and without his permission, but knowing of his disgrace in the town, Emma took the situation in hand and was ready with a fait accompli for when he returned. She had solved three problems with one sweep, running the Emporium, selling the *Advertiser*, and a drunken husband. Oh dear! She quickly corrected herself. 'Damaged husband, of course,' she murmured.

As she returned to the manse, the smile on her face reflected her determination to put her proposals into effect, including confronting her 'damaged' spouse when he arrived home.

One more task remained for Emma in this most productive of mornings, and she made for the office of Clegg the Undertaker. Clegg stood behind his counter reading the latest issue of the *Standard*.

'I have some private words to say to you, Clegg, so perhaps you will close shop for a few minutes.' A puzzled Clegg changed the door sign to 'Closed.'

'You know that my husband is a strong Temperance supporter and only rarely does he drink alcohol himself, so I was astonished when I received him after the cricket match with his nose broken and a strong smell of brandy on his breath. I have heard the Brandish Harvest Ale is almost as weak as water and harvest workers can drink a gallon a day with no effect, so how did he become so drunk with lemon barley water topped up with the ale when he was leading the singing of *Onward Christian Soldiers*? You were the one person who topped-up his drink when the lemon squash was finished and you gave it to him while he was singing. What else did you give him?'

Emma's looked sternly and directly into the face of the undertaker and saw that the suspicions mentioned by her friend, Chapman, were correct. Clegg slumped forward and lowered his head, a stronger admission of guilt than any words.

'It was supposed to be a joke. When I carried the glass to the barrel of ale Rupert Brandish gave me a small flask of brandy to add to the drink as a bit of fun, he said. It certainly made your husband jollier and readier to join in the high-jinks after the meal. Everyone thought it a great laugh.'

'But why did you do it? What has he ever done to you?'

'Well things have not been going so well since he arrived. He has cut my money for looking after the church now that he has stopped morning services when he goes to look after his newspaper. What's more, with bigger crowds on Sunday it makes more work to get things clean and tidy afterwards. Bertram has really made my work more difficult. It was much better for me with the minister before him.'

'So you told Methodist Headquarters in London of his drinking at the regatta.'

'Yes, Mrs. Moorehouse, I did…and I am very sorry. I did not expect it to go so far.' Emma turned on her heel and walked out without another word, anxious not to show the tears that formed; not wishing to make matters worse with this sour undertaker.

Chapter 12

TABLE MANNERS

Mrs. Dorkins put her head round the dining room door. 'The soup is getting cold. Shall I serve it now?'

'Yes, please, Mrs. Dorkins, go ahead. We have already waited half-an-hour for my husband and frankly I do not know where he is nor when he will return.'

Alarm showed on the face of both girls and they looked to their mother for reassurance. Nevertheless, the warm mulligatawny soup was served. But after no more than two sips, they heard a key in the front door and Mrs. Dorkins asking who wanted to enter, then a gasp! The door of the dining room opened and a man in a brown tweed travelling suit with brown shoes and a sticky bandage on his nose came in and sat down.

'I hope I am not too late. Thank you for waiting.'

'Papa.' This from Alice. Then, 'Papa?' queried both girls.

Then their mother. 'Bertie. Where have you been? What have you been doing? Why are you here now?' She thought of the day's events.

'First things first. Let Mrs. Dorkins bring in the beef and then I will tell you the exciting news.' So the family had to try to eat whilst their famished father gobbled up his dinner before starting his explanation.

'Well then? What has happened to you?' Emma sounded concerned, as well she might be. 'Are you ill or feverish? Where have you been?'

'Sorry to have not told you but I realised that after my foolishness my work here was tainted, so I dashed up to London to apologise. It occurred to me in a vision that this was the best thing for me to do. So, first thing this morning I went down to the station and caught the milk train to London. It arrived about eight o'clock but I had to wait at Church House for Grimes to arrive. He was busy and could not see me until midday.'

'What did you do there?'

'I washed in some water in the railway cloakroom but I could not clean the blood from my clothes. So I went out and bought a new suit. Well, not actually new. I exchanged my bloody one for a second-hand clean one. Brown and smart.' And some brown shoes. I thought these went very well together. Then at twelve I knocked on his door and told Grimes that I wanted to apologise to the Church and repair any damage. Grimes went on for a long time telling me of the seriousness of my ways, but that our God is a God of forgiveness following repentance. So, after saying a prayer together he told me the Church's decision.'

'Yes?' 'Yes?' 'Yes?' Said the three members of his family.

'I have been given a new Missionary post in Australia. We are all going to…a circuit near Brisbane.' He fell silent.

Alice put her hands to her face gave a little moan, and rushed out of the room.

Emma was horrified. 'We must talk about this tomorrow

morning over breakfast Bertie, you are upsetting your girls.'

By now Florence was weeping and sniffling into her handkerchief. 'I don't even know what you're talking about.' She left the room to comfort her sister.

At breakfast the next morning Emma steeled herself to break the latest news concerning their daughters. She had rehearsed her speech to herself beforehand. It was to go, 'Bertie, there's something you should know before you make any more plans. Last night, Alice told me that she is expecting a baby and so it will be impossible for her to leave here now, especially to go to Australia. There will already be the terrible disgrace here in the town with this baby, your whole congregation will know about it, and how will you face them? We must do the right thing.'

But when Bertram came into the room, all Emma's planned speech disappeared, and she blurted out, 'Alice is having a baby and will not be going to Australia. What are we going to do?'

Bertram fell into a chair.

'Whaaaat! Well, she can leave this house at once. She can go to one of those Catholic Church places for 'fallen' women like her. Today. As soon as she is packed. That's what! She can go to another part of the country now, before news of her disgrace spreads around the town. That's what we can do!'

'Hussy,' Bertram shouted at the doorway as the two girls came in. 'How dare you disgrace the good name of Moorehouse like this? Things are bad enough here already!'

Alice burst into tears and Florence went across to comfort her. Then Emma went over and put her arms around them both. Bertram did not know what to do so he went to the window and stared out scowling and muttering to himself.

Emma broke away from her sobbing children and touched Bertram's arm.

'Now listen Bertie, things may not be that bad. Alice wants to marry the father, Richard Hyatt, and I think this could be arranged in about a month, God willing. Let me see if I can save the situation so that people here believe Alice is marrying her gentleman because he lives and works here and cannot move to Brisbane. How about that?'

Bertram turned around and Alice stopped crying, lowered her head and smiled at her mother. Bertram nodded and straightened himself up in his new brown suit.

'Yes, that will do, if you can arrange things quickly. I'll tell the Church that you will be joining me later, the girls too.'

Emma took charge. 'Good, let me make the arrangements for the wedding with Richard Hyatt and make it a grand town affair so that you may leave the town with your head in the air feeling proud of your daughter and family. We will follow you later in the year as and when we can.'

She then went on to describe her new relationship with the Emporium and Mr. Chapman's commitments as mayor.

'Mr. Chapman is very busy looking after town matters and he needs someone to look after The Emporium, so he has asked me to keep an eye on things for him. I have said that I would and I can't let him down now that I have promised. I can look after Alice at the same time. Anyway, it will take you some time to settle in and find somewhere for us to live.'

Bertram nodded. The women of the family then left the room to talk things over in Emma's bedroom.

Alice told them, 'I think Richard will be surprised… No, I mean pleased, with the news.'

Chapter 13

DING, DONG

Wearing her best Sunday hat and light summer coat, Emma made her way to the starting point of her wedding round, making decisions as she took her usual walk through the town.

First stop, Hyatt's Butchers at the other end of the High street.

'I want a word with your father, Richard,' she told the astonished young man.

Later on, emerging from the back office, she gave him a firm stare as she walked past, only pausing to turn to his father to say, 'You will make sure we have a proper wedding breakfast, Mr. Hyatt, please.'

'Of course,' said the bewildered butcher. As he wiped his hands on his apron he beckoned his son into the back room.

'Richard, come back here!' (Some shouting ensued.)

Finally, Emma approached Mr. Chapman to tell him of Bertram's departure following the wedding, at which he was traditionally bound to give the bride away. Mr. Chapman would be delighted to attend.

'May I take a few more moments of your time on this busy day?' Mr. Chapman added, making sure the door of the office was shut.

'If you don't mind my asking you a personal question, but where are you going to live if you stay in the town with your daughter and her baby, and do not go to Brisbane. Where will you live?'

Emma had not considered this difficulty yet, but the worry was clear as she put her hand up to her face.

'Oh dear, I have not thought of that yet. We shall have to make way for the new minister, of course. He will need to live in the manse. What shall I do?'

'Forgive my presumption, but I have a suggestion for you to consider and one that might fit in with some plans I have. In the strictest confidence I can tell you that I am going to visit my brother in Ottawa. He's trying to set up a similar business to mine and has asked me to help, but the mayoral obligation has rather delayed things. What with the nonsense between the Brewery and the Temperance people, I dare not leave the town in this state. It looks as though this may be resolved when it's Climand's turn to be mayor next year. What's more, old Brandish has gout, so he will not interfere. He may even be going to Bournemouth for a short stay. So, if I can find someone to look after the business here, I plan to go to Canada myself. My brother certainly needs an extra pair of hands and has already asked me to go.

'This is very hush-hush, for the present, but…' and Chapman took a deep breath and looked at Emma. '…I would like you to look after things here while I am away.'

He looked as though he had shed a huge load from his mind. 'There! And I thought you might like to take over my rooms here above the shop whilst I am gone. I need someone I can trust and you have had time to see how things go here.'

Emma was staggered and looked for somewhere to sit down.

'I'm very flattered, but are you sure I could do things as you want them?'

'Of course I am. You have the right style for our business and the staff are very happy to work with you.'

'This sounds a wonderful plan to me. If you think I could do it, I want to accept, but I must talk it over with Bertie first, and I must make sure Alice is married properly. I'll tell you of our decision tomorrow.'

She rose with a slight tremble and made her way back to the manse.

On reaching home she could not contain all of the excitement of the day, so she went straight to Bertram's study where a large map of Australia was spread on his desk.

He looked up as she entered. 'Australia is such a big place, and Brisbane is so far away, I'm having second thoughts about going. It will be such a wrench for you and Florence, and quite dangerous being surrounded by all those convicts.'

Emma concurred without really knowing any of these details. She had thought that it was probably a bit like India where she had spent her girlhood, and of which she retained one or two pleasant memories.

Reality reared its ugly head.

Bertram went on. 'But we must leave this house and you have nowhere else to go.'

She agreed, almost unbelieving of what she was hearing.

'In any case I would not wish to leave Alice at a time

when every girl needs her mother,' she told her husband. 'I think it's my duty to remain to look after her and the baby. Perhaps it would be better if you went on ahead to settle into your life and surroundings, and we will arrive in due course.'

'What will you do here then, darling?'

'Don't worry about Florence and me, something will turn up for us, I'm sure of that.' This was the ideal time to tell Bertie of Chapman's offer.

'The Emporium needs me. Mr. Chapman has some rooms above the shop that I could use. Florence too, perhaps.' She smiled at him.

Emma had expected this to be a difficult conversation, but her husband replied, 'That is probably the best way to go then. I will go on ahead and you can come when you are ready.'

The next morning, again wearing her best straw hat and a light summer coat, Emma put the rest of her plans into effect. First stop was All Saints Church where Reverend Palmer was in the middle of preparing for his Sunday duties.

'A wedding on a Wednesday afternoon in two weeks' time. Bertie leaving for Australia, you say. We will miss your daughters in the choir.'

'Yes. But they will remain in the town with me for a while and I'm sure they would still enjoy the Temperance choir if other duties allowed. We would like you to take the service in All Saints where Alice will be marrying Richard Hyatt, the butcher's son. We hoped that you could arrange for the Temperance choir to sing at the service. And,' she added, 'perhaps arrange the bells.'

Secretly, the Reverend Palmer was delighted with the news, although somewhat surprised at the timing. A slight smile indicated his understanding of timings of this sort.

'What a surprise.' He glowed. 'A Temperance choir

wedding in the town. How nice.'

A quick stop at the Assembly Rooms to clear the Wednesday afternoon and evening for the wedding breakfast. The steward asked if it was to be 'A Harvest Ale do, or not,' and on being told 'not' he agreed to make available a large quantity of Temperance Ladies' lemonade, a drink now famous in the town. Emma said that this was absolutely splendid.

Emma then approached Mr. Chapman to ask if he would attend as guest of honour. He told her he'd be delighted to come and he would certainly come wearing his chain of office if he had been sworn-in as mayor by that time. Emma ticked him off her list but did not forget to search for a roll of cream coloured silk in the Emporium which she thought would be ideal for the bride's dress. She sighed as she thought of what might have been under different circumstances when she could have chosen white as the dress colour.

She pulled herself together, 'And a piece of blue silk for the bridesmaid.'

Another thing for her to consider. Bertie must have something to wear if he was to give his daughter away, something without blood on it and not brown. A quick visit to the Men's Department, where she told Mr. Spring, the senior staff member, to search for something ready-made. This would avoid Bertie having to visit the clerical tailors in London thus saving time and money.

She recalled the conversation with Mr. Chapman. Perhaps Bertie hadn't heard of the offer for the *Advertiser* yet but he could certainly afford a new black suit if the sale had gone through.

But events were moving fast. While Emma was making her arrangements, Bertram had received a call from the

Town Clerk and was surprised that it was known how much he had originally paid for the newspaper, and was delighted to accept this sum back from the clerk. No questions were posed concerning the future policy of the paper, but he assumed that in the short-term Mayor Chapman would try to inject a Temperance hue to the contents of the merged publication. Not that Bertram had any illusions that this outcome would last very long. The brewing clique would soon influence the editorial and advertising policy of the now joint paper. On his knees that night, Bertram asked forgiveness for letting down the Church by his selling this Methodist voice!

Emma was surprised to learn that all of the townsfolk to whom she spoke were delighted with the news, although eyebrows were raised on hearing of the shortness of the notice. The reason that the Church needed Bertram in Brisbane for a challenging assignment was accepted as an explanation. Most surprised of all was Richard who had learnt the news from an angry father. Fortunately, his mother was more understanding, and rummaged in her jewelry box for a ring of her mother's to be presented to Alice as a symbol of the engagement to her son.

It was no surprise then, when the 'soon to be' groom, hair brushed and wearing a clean shirt, appeared on the front step of the manse asking to see his beloved. Mrs Dorkins gave him a wink and called for Alice to come down to greet her husband to be.

Alone in the sitting room, Richard started to list the questions he wanted to ask whilst trying to make sense of the earlier events. He tried to look aggrieved and angry, ready to demand how he had been forced into this position. But Alice entered, looking radiant, and he forgot his prepared speech.

'Don't you think it's a brilliant idea?' And she put her arms around his neck.

'Pa was going to take Florence and me to Australia with mother and we would never have seen each other again. I had to do something and, knowing the feelings in this town towards unmarried mothers, I thought if I said I was having a baby we would have to get married...I mean...' She paused and looked into his eyes, 'We did talk about it. Didn't we?'

'Well...yes.'

'You haven't changed your mind, have you?'

'Well...No. Only not quite so soon. I thought we were too young. And what's this about a baby?'

'Of course there isn't one...yet. That must be our secret, but I had to lie to convince Papa I couldn't go to Australia with him.' A few tears. 'Or we would never see each other again.' A sob. 'Don't you want to marry me then?' Another sob.

Richard was quite overcome by this tactic and did not know what to say, so he reached into his pocket and found his grandmother's ring.

'I've brought you this.' He blushed as he produced the flashing stones.

'Oh Richard, I do love you so.' Alice cried among the tears, as she put her arms around him and kissed him again.

Richard thought that this was not such a bad idea after all.

'I love you too.' He meant it.

'I'll have to buy a new suit.' And he meant that too.

Later that evening Alice and Florence were sitting in front of the bedroom mirror, each brushing the other's hair while reflecting on the coming big event, as they prepared for bed.

'It really is a lovely ring.' Florence told her sister. 'I hope to have one as nice when I become engaged.' She sighed. 'But it'll be some time before that happens. Peter doesn't want me to go to Brisbane and he says he doesn't want to lose me. And I am really fond of him. Anyway, I don't want to go at all if you won't be there. He's been busy making other arrangements for me.' She paused. 'But I haven't told Mama and Papa yet.'

'You sly little thing,' said her sister. 'I didn't think that you were getting engaged. When did this happen?'

'It hasn't yet, but Peter is making plans for me.'

'Plans? Plans? What are you talking about?'

'He found me a little job in Timothy Whites where he's training to be a dispenser at the shop that's managed by his uncle. They are to open a lending library in the upstairs of their shop and they need someone to stamp the date in the books as they are lent out and to collect the fines if they are late being returned, that sort of thing. I love books and I'd really like to do it as a paid job. What's more, Peter's aunt and uncle have a spare room I could rent for half a crown a week, so I could save some money for my wedding while I was there. Their house is near to the Emporium so I could meet Mama whenever I liked. She would like that.'

Alice was amazed at this sudden news and stopped brushing Florence's hair.

'And when is this all going to take place.'

'Not for some time yet. First Peter has to complete his training to be a shop chemist,and then we have to find a house to live in. In a couple of years, I should think. So you see I can't go to Brisbane either.' A moment's reflection, 'But don't tell Mama.' She sighed, 'I like this little town and the people here, and I really don't want to leave.'

A fortnight later all of Emma's plans came to fruition.

All Saint's Church had fresh flowers, the Temperance Choir had rehearsed one of its anthems, extra chairs had been found for them, and Reverend Palmer had chosen the right words to express his delight at being invited to conduct this service for two members of his choir. Meanwhile Emma had found suitable 'mother of the bride' clothes at the Emporium, and had bought a fashionable new hat from the town milliner.

The bride looked magnificent in her sari-like cream silk dress, enhanced with a slight bulge at the front with a little padding provided by Mrs Dorkins who knew about such occasions, and also what the town would expect. The bridesmaid, Florence, also looked stunning in her blue silk dress and smiled from time to time at the best man, Peter, who smiled back in return. Several of the ladies from the Temperance choir whispered to each other how different the butcher's son looked standing at the altar, upright and handsome in his new finery. One or two exhaled small sighs of envy. Mr. Chapman rattled his chain of office across another new waistcoat when he sat next to Emma as they watched Bertram, also newly suited, bring up the bride on his arm.

Tears came into all of the married feminine eyes of the congregation, each one mistily recalling their own personal memories of days gone by.

Alter the Palmerian oration of some length, and the signing of the register, the bride and groom went by pony and trap to the Assembly Rooms where an appropriate meaty banquet was displayed. Pork and beef, pies and pasties, plum puddings and blancmange were consumed by all the guests. By this time they had been joined by several prominent tradesmen of the town, and even Rupert Brandish was seen kissing the bride on the cheek. Mr. Climand was noted handing over a small leather purse that chinked.

At the weekend, the *Advertiser and Standard* produced a list of all of those present, each with their wedding gift. Miss McGregor had donated a thistle decorated vase and the fellow pupils had embroidered a fine tablecloth using a riverine theme. The list covered two whole pages but the front page was made over to the following announcement:

To All of our Readers
It is with great pleasure that we can announce
the Merger of the two newspapers of the town
into one. In future this will be known as
The Standard and Advertiser.

We shall continue to offer coverage of news
of all groups of citizens and denominations
and to fairly report all Town events.

The rest of the page was taken up by a large advertisement for Brandish Ales.

Chapter 14

INTERMISSION

Two days after the wedding, Mrs Dorkins came into the drawing room where Emma was sewing.

'Excuse me ma'am. May I have a private word?'

Emma nodded to the chair opposite. 'Please take a seat, Mrs Dorkins.'

'I'll stand if you don't mind, ma'am.' Here there was a short pause and a clearing of the throat. 'When we came here you asked me to arrange the washing and ironing of all of the linen in the house and I have always done this. But I feel I should tell you from what I know that neither of your daughters is expecting a baby.'

Silence for a few moments as the news filtered through the barrier of disbelief, then Emma lowered her head and said, 'Thank you, Mrs Dorkins, I hope that we can keep that information between us.'

A quick curtsey of understanding from the message bearer, and then she left the room.

The happy couple had spent their honeymoon night

in a room at the Bridge Hotel but left for Richard's home prior to his restarting work in the family shop on Monday. Alice was offered a position of assistant cashier in the shop as a short-term measure and took over the cash counter from Richard's mother on the first Monday.

On the day following the wedding, a gentleman in a loose brown suit and brown shoes was seen alone, boarding the early milk train on route to Southampton. He carried a suitcase in which was packed the smart new black suit worn when he gave his elder daughter away at her wedding, a symbol of his optimism for the future.

As the train pulled away, Bertram could not resist looking back to the bridge from where he had watched the elephants bathing in the cool green water, and where he had made such bright plans for his family in this new town. How much more water would flow under the bridge before they were united again, who knows where, but maybe in Brisbane?

He need not have worried.

Shortly after his landing in Australia, the monthly letter from Emma, which had been forwarded from Brisbane to his new circuit about one hundred and fifty miles inland, told him of the progress each of his family members was making. When he finally received it, memories of past happiness returned for a while. Eventually he became relieved they had not travelled with him, as the realities of his own situation became clearer. The tiny hut which was his home and the centre of his Church Circuit was at the limit of the new settlers' penetration into virgin country. Slowly the realisation came to Bertram that this was the Church's way of reflecting disapproval. Grimes had known about the difficulties of this posting and it was his Methodist way of punishment for past failures. It was not the harshness of the semi-barren location that concerned Bertram, he was tough enough to overcome any difficulty with God's help, but the thought that his family would have been expected to live in these harsh conditions made his anger rise. He found thoughts of his lovely wife and the elegant ladies that his daughters had become, having to endure the realities of this location, being punished for what they had not done, utterly beyond acceptance. The reality of the situation would prevent Emma and his daughters from coming here at all; maybe this was the real – and intended – punishment. Monthly letters from Emma were still loving and full of anticipation of their life together. What was he to do? When he wrote back to his wife his tone was deliberately cautious, avoiding all mention of the home they would be sharing and never telling her of the heat and the effect of the dryness on the local animals and plants. He could not mention the word 'drought' which was now in its third year and which threatened the survival of every living thing, yet this was the reality which dominated his existence.

Chapter 15

LETTERS

It must be said that the town, back in England, under the control of Mayor Climand – who was the obvious replacement for the missing doctor Redesdale – began to improve. The fact that he had started to build a new row of high-class villas on a piece of land owned by All Saints church, with the first being for his own occupancy, drew his attention to some of the deficiencies of the town. Always a stickler for health matters and better standards of hygiene, the new mayor started, with some gusto, to tackle the long-standing problems of town cleanliness. Two cholera cases started his drive for a fever hospital, which was built a mile out of town with the help of some Masonic money. As it was finished, the first smallpox cases were discovered, but were immediately isolated in the new unit. The relief felt by many was translated into additional votes for him at the next election. A new road and pavement through the middle of the shopping area at Christmas time, which was normally a sea of mud at that time of year, drew more plaudits.

Townsfolk were noticeably relieved when it was announced in *The Advertiser and Standard* that at the Council New Year dinner, Mr. Climand and Mr. Brandish senior had shaken hands and each had made a conciliatory speech.

The new mayor's position was helped by government extensions of the town boundary southwards, taking in areas for good building land. As each extension was approved by water companies and gas providers, they extended their networks, and these modern developments attracted a more professional type of resident. Such newcomers, while not usually strong Temperance supporters, were, in the main, solid Liberal voters and they found Climand's improvements attractive. The population of the old town clustered round the public houses was eventually matched by the newcomers, who then became the voting majority. This led to Climand's position as mayor being made stronger, so that his position was eventually renewed for a total of six terms of office.

Emma watched the changing face of the town with interest and also with some pleasure from her chair, still placed just inside the entrance of the Emporium, especially as the cashier Mr. Spring, presented her with the takings, each day swollen by the newcomers.

Reports to Mr. Chapman were glowing confirmation of his choice of manageress and he reflected his appreciation with regular bonuses. The new family business in Ottawa was proving troublesome and he felt obliged to remain in Canada to bring about some improvements there. That made trustworthy hands at home very important to give him time to solve his immediate problems.

Emma had had none of the expected increased family demands yet; she merely raised an eyebrow when she glanced at her daughter's waistline. Alice just raised her eyebrow in return. There was much more to keep Alice occupied at home as her husband needed to spend more and more time with his father's butchery business. Mr. Hyatt senior had moved to live next door to the building that had been taken over by an out-of-town fishmongers chain. This new fish business received supplies on the first train from Hull each morning and Richard's father offered to take over the running of the trade for the new owners, Mac Fisheries, as, of course, the bigger company had taken away any freshwater trade he had previously enjoyed. Richard ran the butchery business with the help of Alice, who sat in the cash cubicle where she took the customers' money and gave them change. Later, when a friend of his father approached Richard and asked if he had thought about becoming a Freemason, as this was the normal practice for sons of Masons, Richard said he would ask his father what would be appropriate.

Alice was even busier when they decided to sell Dorkin's homemade pies, hams, and other cooked meats. She loved watching Richard making such a success of his trade and she enjoyed working with him and mixing with the customers from the town. Secretly she was pleased that the sale of eels had moved next door since she still had the vision of the horse's head episode.

Florence moved into the rooms above the Emporium with her mother but she did not take up her mother's offer of a job there. The dream her friend from the picnic had was still in her mind. Peter was always the more studious of the pair of young Temperance choir tenors, and when Timothy Whites moved into a vacant shop in the town, he immediately found a position as a trainee pharmacist. This meant his going to London from time to time for classes and exams, but his future was secure. In this position in the new store he had learnt of the plan to open a lending library in the upstairs rooms and that they would be needing an assistant librarian to stamp the books, take the money, and collect the fines for late returns. Florence seemed the ideal person for this work and obtained the assistant librarian position in the Timothy Whites branch. She was delighted, particularly as the couple could spend their lunch times together every day and sometimes they would join Emma at the Temperance café. From her first wages, Florence took two shillings and sixpence to pay for one week's advance rent for the room in Richard's uncle and aunt's house.

Each lunch time, Emma would walk to the Temperance café where she had a favourite corner seat, and after a sandwich or a pastry, she would take out her writing pack of paper, envelopes and stamps and use her indelible pencil to write a letter to Bertram.

Town Temperance Café

My Dearest Bertie,
I could not sit by the river today as the workmen are finally making the new promenade that Mr. Climand has promised for so long. I am sure it will be very nice and everyone should now get a good view of the bridge you loved so much. So I am in the coffee shop as usual.

You will not be surprised to learn that Florence has a position now in the upstairs Lending Library at Timothy Whites.

She always was a keen reader and I think that she is expected to tell customers what she thinks of any new books that they have. So this is ideal for her. Between you and me, I think that she also likes to be near to her friend Peter who also works in the shop downstairs. He seems a serious lad and is studying to be a pharmacist. Good luck to him I say.

I called in at Hyatts but it was so busy that Alice

could not spare the time for a chat, and I could not see much of her now that she sits in the cash booth. I just pointed down to her tummy and winked at her and she shook her head. So, 'no news from the front' as they say in South Africa. (What a terrible situation there.)

I am keeping pretty well and things are extremely busy at the Emporium. Not quite so for me as I just advise ladies and supervise. Mr. Chapman must be pretty pleased with me as he has just sent me another bonus. I do not think things are so good in Ottawa where there are a lot of Americans coming in.

I think he must not be too well as his writing is a little shaky these days. Did I tell you that now that I have some money I am putting it in the new Trustee Savings Bank brought in by Mr. Climand. You can borrow even more if you are going to buy a house and pay it back later. What a good idea this is. Of course Mr. Climand thinks so as he is building the houses. I visited one the other day and it had a nice kitchen and indoor facilities.

But I seem to have rambled on without saying how much I worry about you and how you are getting on. Your news is so scarce and I am sure you are having trouble settling in. We pray for you every night that you are not troubled by illness or anything else. Please tell me if you need anything from here in the way of comforts etc. I will send what you ask although the ships seem to take forever.

Well my dear, the coffee is cold and my work awaits. The girls and I miss you terribly. Keep well and I will send you news of your grandson??? When there is any.

With all of my love,
Emma xxx

My Dearest Emma,

Your news is so precious and I wait each day at the gate for your next letter. I miss you so much.

As you will know from my earlier epistle from the ship, I should be based here in Brisbane, or, more correctly, I am about 150 miles inland. This is good farming country, I am told, but we are very short of water and the plants, except eucalyptus, are all dried up. My poor parishioners are desperate as their cattle are dying. Yesterday the temperature was over 100 degrees with a wind blowing sand everywhere, eyes, nose, and throat. A person could easily die if he is caught out of doors.

The farmers here are badly in need of help, but not the sort that I can give. I mainly take funerals and even help with the grave digging. What we really want are wells and irrigation but the government has this problem everywhere and our needs are down the list. Tomorrow I am going with a group to Brisbane to tell the government just how bad things are. (And to the Post Office.)

I take prayers with my people when I can visit them, but really they are much dispersed, and although the Church has provided me with a site and piece of land, I have no building except for my small home.

I miss you all so much and hunger for your news, being much relieved none of it is bad.

Save for that naughty Alice. God bless her. Finally, I have discovered a ship that is returning to England soon. I hope it will carry this letter.

I love you all and miss you most, my dear wife.
Love, Bertram

P.S. The Captain has a spare space. My work here is done and I am coming home.

This was the last letter that Emma received from Bertram for three years. After several requests to the Methodist Church authorities in London, she was told of his sudden departure on the mail boat, accompanied by a request to keep them informed if he should show up in the town. They added, however, that due to the war currently being fought in South Africa, the mail boat had been instructed to unload its cargo at Cape Town and to return home to Australia on war business. No information could be obtained concerning the passengers.

Then…nothing…For two years…Nothing. Nothing!!!

Wessels Becke, May 16th
Now I am pressed into The Bucks Yeomanry and have borrowed this pencil to send you a note with our runner. I have no news of you, my dear, but sent several notes saying I was coming home. But landing without any money, I was fortunate to meet an acquaintance from church who took me under his care until I was well enough to travel, and I am with his regiment as padre. We are on the march through Elandslaagte, clearing out the country of Boers, but the artful devils don't stop for us to get anywhere near them as they clear off as soon as they see our advance guard. We did 20 miles across country from Sunday at 5 p.m. until 11 p.m. Monday, with just a few hours' sleep in a mealie field, without tents or blankets for the last 5 days. I can tell you it is not playing at war out here, although we have had no serious fighting but jolly hard grafting. But I am now in

good health and hard as nails and am glad to be here if only for the experience. I hope to be able to come home after we have captured Pretoria. My unit will move in half an hour so I must send my love to yourself and the girls. Your affectionate husband. Bertie.

Again…Nothing.

After three years without any news at all, Emma was staggered to receive the above letter in the post from Cape Town, from where it had been forwarded by the regimental post office. After reading this emotive epistle from her husband Emma decided to show it to her daughters, and after visiting Florence in the Timothy Whites Library and then Alice at Hyatt's butchers, she arranged to meet in the Temperance café for them all to read the letter at leisure together and to try and squeeze as much information from it as possible. Also, to decide what to do next. It emerged that the Bucks Yeomanry had already left for home and although the sergeant in charge at the depot had heard of their temporary padre he thought that he had been left at Cape Town since no berth had been provided for him on the boat home.

The family agreed that Emma should send a letter to Bertie addressed to the Methodist Church in Cape Town in the hope that her husband would call in. There was no news and no reply. Bertie may not have received the letter, nor even have been in the town, but what else could she do. The three ladies went back to their shop duties whist waiting for more news.

Other members of the Militia were found and questioned, and one remembered a funeral service performed in the field for one of their comrades that fell to a sniper's bullet. He was buried by their padre whose description resembled Bertie, but he had no name for the reverend. It seemed that penniless Bertram had remained in South Africa.

The next day Emma awoke early with a start. Of course, the person who would know would be Captain Brandish, he was in charge of the town section of Yeomanry, and he must remember Bertram and would know where her husband had moved to. She visited the brewery as soon as her duties at the Emporium allowed. Rupert was busy but would see her at midday.

'As far as I know, Hopwell found your husband lying on the side of the dock at Capetown, possibly drunk. Anyway, Hopwell put him on the provisions wagon and brought him to the regimental camp where he was given a wash down and some food. We moved out a week later to chase the Boers, but your husband was slow and holding the men back so I sent him on Boer patrol to round up the families and that was the last I saw of him. I suppose he could have gone native, but I never saw him again…Sorry Mrs Moorehouse.'

Emma was distraught, but what else did she expect? She made her negative report to her two daughters and only then did she break down into tears.

'Oh poor, poor, Bertie,' she sobbed. 'What did they do to you?'

Mrs Dorkins was called to see her home and to make her a cup of tea.

Chapter 16

LOST AND FOUND

'Mrs Moorehouse, there's a foreign man at the side door who says he needs to see you.'

The junior assistant from the haberdashery came up to Emma's usual chair at the entrance to the ladies department of The Emporium, showing signs of modest haste.

'What does he want? Did he say?'

'No ma'am, he looks very brown and is carrying rolls of leather, but he would not tell me what he wanted. He just said he wanted to see you urgently, that was all.'

Emma made her way to the commercial travellers' entrance of the store.

'Well then, my man, what do you want to see me about?' Her approach to the man who stood at the doorway with the bright sunlight behind him, was to put it mildly, brusque, irritated at his impertinence at taking up her valuable time. He did not give a good impression, heavily bearded and wearing a brown suit. His leather hat was in one hand and he held a roll of leather in the other.

'Hello, Emma. I hoped you might want to talk about our lost years.'

The shock, once she had recognised his voice, caused her to stumble forward a little, so the stranger stepped forward to steady her with his hand on her shoulder, dropping his hat in the process. She looked at the blue eyes set in the wrinkled brown face with its bushy beard and tobacco-stained moustache.

'Bertie! Is it you? Where have you been? It's been years since you were here. What have you been doing? I had your last letter from South Africa two years ago and the girls and I thought you had died.'

'Well I nearly did, once or twice, but The Lord saw me through, so here I am. Let us go somewhere so that I can say how sorry I am for not writing more often and tell you why it was impossible for me.'

Emma quickly called in at Hyatts and Alice arranged for Mrs Dorkins to look after 'Little Bertie,' as she had named her new son, and Emma asked her to call in at Timothy Whites library to gather her sister so that they could all meet at the Temperance café to learn and exchange all the news. There was a rather embarrassing atmosphere at first because the two girls did not recognise their bearded and tanned father, but Emma explained that long hours in the South African sun had bronzed and withered Bertie's appearance, but his voice certainly was the same, neither had those eyes changed.

Bertram's questions concerning the town, Alice's husband, and his new grandson, the fate of the newspaper, and the new Methodist minister, immediately told them that this was the same man. But it was Florence who asked the question they all wanted to know the answer to.

'Tell us Papa, where have you been all these years?'

Bertram took a long breath, then asked if they minded if he smoked a cigar, and without waiting for a response, said, 'Well, darlings, it's a long story.'

Emma interrupted him, 'Not now girls, let us get Papa settled first. You can come and share my house if you wish, Bertie. I have a little terraced place that I am buying from Mr. Climand and I have a spare room you can use whilst you are here. When you are cleaned up a bit I will ask the girls and their men – husband in Alice's case – to come to dinner, and then you can tell us all about your travels with the army. Oh yes, we did get one letter from South Africa, but nothing since. We shall have one of Mrs Dorkins's pies. That'll help you remember a bit about our home here in the old days. I'm afraid we thought you were dead…dear.'

This last word was carefully chosen as Emma repeated their fears, and she needed a small pause to select the most appropriate affectionate term for her lost husband as they made their way to her new home on the edge of the town.

'Well I can tell you that that was nearly true after that miserable captain of the Brisbane ship dumped me on the quay at Cape Town. I had been ill on board with dysentery and fever, so when he received instructions to return to Australia for war duties he put me ashore and left me there in spite of my having paid him for my passage to England. He kept the money I had paid him, so I crawled into the shade of a warehouse and lay with my head on my clothes sack and would have died there and then if Corporal Hopwell had not recognised me and taken me on his regimental provision cart back to the Army camp outside of the town. Hopwell had been in our town Temperance choir and was a friend of Peter and Richard – I think they were tenors together, anyway he had attended to sing at your wedding Alice, although I did not notice him then, and he was in the choir at St Mary's. He picked me up and took me to the regimental billet of the Bucks Yeomanry, he gave me some water and saved my life. I am sure of that and I shall be always grateful.'

They had reached the front door and Bertie was shown into the spare room. Emma then brought up a bowl and some water, before returning to the Emporium for a clean shirt and suit of clothes. When they saw him next, everyone tried not to notice Bertram's shrunken frame in clothes made to his previous measurements.

Both Alice and Florence remembered Hopwell from their days in the choir and their men, too, had memories of their friend with his fine voice.

The family group were interested in what had changed their father into this brown facsimile of the man they had known and each started to ask all of these outstanding questions at once.

Bertram took on a more serious tone as he settled into his chair and resumed his tale.

'I was just starting to recover when the regiment received orders to move up country. I had no money, and Hopwell was feeding me from leftover scraps from the kitchen. But Captain Brandish solved the situation by enabling me to sign on with the Bucks Yeomanry as a padre. He had taken command from Major Grey, you know, and he put me on the ration roll. He did not mention the cricket incident to me except to tell me to teach the troops *Onward Christian Soldiers*, which we sang as we marched through Cape Town towards the railway station.'

The brown man, now shaved and without his beard, but leaving a large moustache, relit his small cigar and took a deep pull on its fragrance.

'I'm not sure I can talk about the next few months. This

was wartime and it was a situation we ought not to be proud of. I think you received one letter from me when our troops were on the move and I followed with the support group. Although we did not catch or shoot any of the enemy, we burnt his farms and crops and of course we seized the women and children. Brandish directed me and eight others to escort these civilians to a wired camp some miles away. I stayed at this civilian prison for two years...as a guard, which was a cruel experience for me. Watching those folk die of hunger and disease...they were only on half-rations you know, and we lost fully half of them when the cholera arrived.'

Bertie put his head in his hands and his cigar ash fell on the table.

'Don't tell us anymore, Bertie.' Emma put her arm around his shoulder.

'You're home now, my dearest,' she continued, as she waved her children and their friends towards the front door.

'Good night, Papa,' Florence whispered, as she and Peter departed.

'Goodnight.' Alice kissed his head as she and Richard left for home.

The Moorehouse family were left to gather other scraps of Bertram's lost years as he slowly tried to accustom himself to his new existence. One fact was certain. The Reverend Bertram Moorehouse was a changed man.

Chapter 17

NEW TOWN

The death of Queen Victoria led to a new feeling of optimism in the town. New trades came from outside, encouraged by the railway. A pleasure steamer had started during the summer to give visitors trips on the beautiful river, and there was talk of a new hotel being built near the station. Everyone was amazed when Grange and Sons, the boat makers, offered river launches powered by electric motors. More shops had opened in the high street for the population which had grown to six and a half thousand. The incoming families bought new houses in the southern suburb on the Methodist side of town, and a fresh young minister, Reverend Grange, had taken care of their spiritual needs.

Bertram only rarely ventured into the town and then mostly to the Temperance café to join Emma for her sandwich lunch. Sometimes, one of his daughters, often Florence, would also join them at lunchtimes when the library at Timothy Whites was closed. She often talked about Peter's pharmacy position there, but occasionally she also told her parents of his visits to meetings in London at the Congregational Memorial Hall, where political meetings were increasingly gathered to promote rights for workers. She travelled up to London with Peter on some Wednesdays and wandered around while he dealt with pharmacy matters, and went to a meeting for the first time to shelter from the rain. There was talk of the formation of a political party to represent them. Peter had hinted that the formation of a branch of the Labour Party in the town might take place, and one evening she had actually attended one of their meetings at the Assembly Rooms. Bertram was confused but told Emma that he thought nothing would come of it. But sitting back in his café seat he noticed that the clientele around him had started all to look a little older. One or two had the start of greying hair.

Since the painful episode at the table, Emma had never questioned her husband further about his experiences in South Africa but, little by little, more details emerged in the course of their conversations, and when she asked him about the bundle of leather pieces he now had placed in the wooden garden shed, he seemed relieved to be able to talk about it.

It appeared that Bertram was not considered a properly-equipped soldier, having had to spend most of his time in bed recovering from his fever, so the regiment's departure for action had not given him enough time to prepare. After the troops set out to follow General Kitchener's orders to harass the Boers, Bertram found that twenty to thirty miles a day had worn out his boots. He was lagging behind the Yeomanry and his feet were bleeding. Hopwell's bandages did not help. It was at this point that Captain Brandish ordered him to join the rearguard to mop up the civilian stragglers, mainly women and children. It was a hard twenty-five miles to the wire-enclosed compound which marked their destination, but the end of the forced march seemed a blessing for guards and prisoners alike. The instruction to only feed the families half-rations of mealie flour and meat with no vegetables or milk, together with tented accommodation and the allocation of one sanitary bucket per tent, soon resulted in outbreaks of illness. Once cholera was identified, deaths rose to as many as twenty-five a day in the camp. This situation continued for two years, including two winters when the camp inmates suffered horribly. Bertram's face told of the misery he had witnessed, and to some extent shared, but he sufficed to say, 'It was a cruel thing to do and it was a disgrace to the Empire.'

He fell silent, seemingly lost for words. Emma broke the silence by pointing to the rolls of leather.

'How did you come by this, then?'

Bertie's face brightened. 'Shortly after our arrival at the camp, a group of native traders approached the wire barrier and offered goods for sale. They also had some food to sell but one of them had animal skins, and after looking at my feet he offered a gazelle skin and a piece of buffalo hide in exchange for the cross around my neck. I insisted on a needle and twine to be included which he passed through the fence to me, and three days later he came back with a small bunch of Zulu herbs which he said I should smoke while I was working. He didn't say why. I'd made a new pair of shoes. This was something of a miracle at the time and I knelt down and gave thanks for my so-far hidden talent. Over the next weeks other guards needed new boots or gaiters which I made with more skins; gazelle, zebra, but mainly springbok. I became the camp bootmaker, even sun hats if I could, and I saved a little cash as well. Of course,

I continued to say prayers on Sundays, even some of the Boer women would stand near at such times and we could sing some hymns together. I was also asked to say prayers for the dead and dying, which I found distressing, but I tried to give comfort where I could. For two years I said prayers and made shoes. God seemed to have chosen me for this. A new mission, you might say.'

Slowly, and over time, Bertram released a little more detail of his life as a concentration camp guard, almost always saying how he missed his home and Emma in particular, but no one had taken care to inform the authorities who he was, nor where he had been sent. No news or letters reached him, and he relied on regimental gossip and rumour concerning the war and the reasons he was placed at the camp. When a peace was signed with the Boers and the camp residents were sent home, Bertram was returned to Cape Town. He was not on the list for embarkation for England; no one spoke on his behalf, and he was left with his leather hides, needles, and shoe-making skills. These talents, plus a small quantity of cash, enabled him to acquire enough money for a ticket home. But he first made sure of his supply of African skins; using credit from Indian merchants, his leather source was then secure for the future. He confessed that he was not sure that he would be welcome after such a long break in communication with Emma and the family, nor even if they were still in the same town. After all, it must have appeared to them that he had abandoned them.

His best hope was that sergeant Hopwell, now wounded, Bertram learned from his fellows, was able to tell Emma of his plight. This message had reached Emma but that was two years before and when he had been able to borrow the pencil stub to send his last hurried note.

But it was enough! Emma had not given up; her

daughters and new grandson had given her the strength to carry on with her life. Chapman's trust in her to run his business while he was in Canada had given her the physical means to acquire a new small house. Chapman himself was able to use his rooms above the Emporium whenever he returned from his business in Toronto and his confidence in the business relationship with Emma had grown. His return visits had however become less frequent once his brother became ill in Ottawa.

During his first weeks of rebuilding his relationship with his wife while lodging with her, Bertram worked at their home while she looked after her business. He begged a piece of wood from Climand's yard and shaped it into a pair of wooden lasts which he then used as models of Emma's feet for his first pair of town shoes. These were sewn from antelope skins and were finally polished by hand with beeswax. Emma was delighted with her surprise gift, recognising the tenderness and plea for forgiveness that had gone into their making. It was with tears in her eyes that she placed them on her feet. The fit was perfect, of course.

'Bertie, they are absolutely beautiful. God has found a way to reward you for all of your suffering by giving you this skill. Bless you, my darling.'

On the following market day, Emma came home in the middle of the day full of excitement.

'Bertie, Bertie,' she called to the outside shed. 'Where are you? I have something to tell you. I have just finished telling Mr. Climand, who is now our mayor, that you have come home and that you would like to set up a shoe shop. He was very interested and suggested that you might like a new space that was left after the demolishing of the Shearer's Arms which was done to make way for the New Town Hall. There's a small square room next to the passageway which now leads to the market place, and he thinks that the Council would let you rent it for your new business. What do you think?'

This was the first hint that Bertram had received that Emma was far ahead of him in this kind of thinking, but he had noticed her worried look concerning his future each time she left for her position at the Emporium. He had not been sure what he wanted to do. In particular, he re-lived the embarrassment of the events that had led to his departure and he worried that his previous church flock would shun him. Perhaps they still thought that he had let them down.

Emma was all encouragement. 'They'll admire you for making a fresh start.'

During the following days the new town cobbler measured his daughter's feet in order to fashion working copies from which he made two pairs of shoes, one from a springbok hide and one from that of a gazelle. Bertram set these polished specimens in the window of the vacant shop while he searched out a signwriter to paint his shop announcement:

Ladies' and gentlemen's hand-crafted footwear
from South African leathers

Emma added the words:

Quality Workmanship Guaranteed

Gossiping with her lady customers at the Emporium, she managed to mention her husband's new business while displaying her own luxurious footwear for them to admire. The interest that created frequently led to orders for similar shoes. No one mentioned the Methodist Church nor its previous minister – nor cricket matches.

Bertie's new business was a success from the first weeks.

Five years on, it was apparent that the town residents had forgotten their previous Methodist minister, and even if faithful members of his congregation recognised him, nobody mentioned his earlier church position.

Bertie discovered that the combined town newspaper had moved from the upper rooms above Butler's chemist shop to new premises next door to the Masonic Hall. But when he eventually paid a visit to place an advertisement for his new business, none of the staff showed any signs of recognition. All of the one-time *Standard* workers were engaged with the new printing machine at the rear of the premises. The advertisement worked well and resulted in more trade for his luxury footwear business. Bertram introduced an additional sales line in hunting boots for the county set, and the purchase of a rotary grinder and polisher speeded up his shoe fabrication enough to employ a young lad, Arthur, to help with the trade.

Emma was able to introduce her newly-found tradesman husband to other important councillors and professional men in the town, and included him as her escort to special events that she attended on behalf of the Emporium. In the absence of Mr. Chapman, she borrowed the Emporium electric launch that had been booked for privileged customers at regatta time to cruise up and down the rowing course with her husband at the helm and their daughters lounging on cushions under the umbrella shade at the rear. Bertram felt the admiring glances, and inwardly told himself that the family had finally 'arrived' in the town.

His three ladies had indeed, each in her own way, been accepted by the townsfolk. Florence was transformed following the visit she had made to London with Peter on her Wednesday day-off; he went to his lecture at the Pharmaceutical Institute while she wandered into the Congregational Memorial Hall. It was not her intention to go inside but the bad weather pushed her to take shelter. Keir Hardie was talking to the Society of Railway Servants about being stronger as a Union, and Florence was won over by his case for the working man. The town where she lived was not reliant on heavy industry, but she saw how domestic servants were exploited, and, in particular, she saw how the farm workers in the region were browbeaten and held by tied cottages. When she met Peter after his lecture she could not stop chattering on about Hardie's tirade of inequalities and the need for a movement to bring better conditions for workers. Her tired friend sank into his seat in the carriage and nodded agreement. After this first visit to the capital, Florence accompanied Peter whenever his chemist's affairs took him there on a Wednesday afternoon, the half-day off for shop workers. He little guessed that this charming friend of his would become a leading figure in the new Labour party that grew up in the town in later years.

Her sister Alice had also become a recognised character in the town, still operating the cash desk at her husband's butcher's shop with her now two young boys being looked after by a doting grandmother, helped by a nursemaid. This allowed Alice to accompany her husband to Masonic dinner events which he regularly attended now that he had been inducted into the local Masonic Lodge as the son of an active Mason. As a leading tradesman in the town, Richard's father had been a member for many years and it had been expected that his son would join the brotherhood at the age of twenty-one. Alice enjoyed these opportunities to meet other wives in the town and often these ladies gave their opinions on town matters when they were without their husbands, notwithstanding the required Temple requirement for an Oath of Silence. Bertram found his daughters' intimate knowledge of the workings of the town helpful when he was setting up his trade, also when he needed their help as he started to pursue another project close to his heart.

It was at a family dinner organised by Emma that he first raised his concerns about fellow ex-soldiers he met in the town from time to time, but it was his encounter with his friend and saviour, sergeant Hopwell, that brought home the sad plight of these discarded men. Hopwell had lost a leg in the war and was able to tell Bertram of several other ex-soldiers living locally who were in a similar plight. These were unemployable, sick men, living in the shadows on scraps and the proceeds of their begging bowls. Bertram suggested that the town should help repay its debts to these heroes by providing them with proper nursing care. Alice asked Richard what would be the best way to do this and he thought that the Masons could help if the right officials were approached. He offered to do this, but Emma said that it would need Brandish money, and probably donations from builder Mayor Climand. Florence thought that a public subscription box could be put in the library to help.

The initiative that started here at the family table was a success and a Masonic-led fund resulted in a special hospital for the wounded from South Africa being built on a plot of land on the southern fringe of the town. Bertram visited these survivors whenever he could and exchanged many tales of the South African campaign with them. He was surprised that very few of them knew of the plight of the abandoned families of the retreating Boer fighters.

Chapter 19

RETRIBUTION

'Nice little place you have here.' Bertram recognised the voice straightaway and turned his head away from the shoe he was polishing at his wheel to confirm that it really was Rupert Brandish, someone he had not seen since the Yeomanry Captain had consigned him to be a guard at the concentration camp in South Africa – nearly three years ago. There was a temptation to tell his visitor something of the hardships and discomfort he had experienced as a result of his experiences at that time.

The words did not come. How much recompense could be gained in this way – and it was a long time ago. The Brandish face was open and unmoving and Bertram guessed that the man at his counter had forgotten the episode. To him, it had been something of a rather minor joke, but for Bertram it had destroyed his Methodist Church career.

'Friends tell me you make a rather good boot,' the visitor commented, 'And I must say that the shoes in the window look rather smart.'

'Yes,' said Bertram, 'It was something I picked up during the war in Africa, and all of my shoes use animal hides from there. They can be turned into something light and handsome, and of course they wear very well.'

'So I have been told. I would like you to make me a pair of your best riding boots, suitable for the hunt, don't y'know. Something smart to catch the eye.'

Bertram swallowed the brusque refusal he was tempted to give and indicated the chair where he placed his clients in order to take their foot measurements. This was required before the creation of a pair of wooden formers, from which he could proceed to turn the chosen leather into comfortable boots. Brandish used the time to look around the shop and noticed the rolls of imported skins standing in the corner, just arrived from Bertram's agent at the Cape.

When Bertram had finished his measurements, Rupert Brandish walked over and examined a few skins. After glancing at several he pulled one out to spread on the counter.

'This has jolly fine markings.' He stroked a rare gazelle pelt, then he gave it a long deep breath with his nose close to it.

'Reminds me of the Karoo desert in bloom.'

'Well the natives have their own way of curing skins there you know, which keeps the leather supple.'

'It will certainly make a handsome pair of boots.' It was agreed that the boots would be delivered to the brewery before the start of the hunting season, but no price was mentioned – the usual form when dealing with the gentry.

Rupert Brandish made no mention of Bertram's escape from Africa nor of the concentration camps during their exchange about hunting boots. Nor was there any reference to his earlier career as a Methodist Minister, or to cricket matches, for which Bertram was grateful.

Brandish pushed his way out through the shop door with a curt, 'Thank-ya.'

Later, Bertram carried this most recent delivery of hides to his smokehouse behind the shop and, after lighting a cigar, he arranged them on the horizontal poles. He lit two sulphur candles, closed the door and retired. This was his usual procedure with hides imported from abroad, although South African leather workers swore that the smoking of a large herb cigar whist working with leather was enough protection from any nasty local diseases.

Emma showed some surprise when she was told of Rupert's visit and of the fact of his apparent ignorance of the fate of his regimental cobbler, but by this time she was aware of the idiosyncrasies of the gentry and their attitudes towards the tradespeople.

Several weeks passed, during which time the family had discussed which church to attend together on Sundays. Bertram felt that his reappearance at the Methodist chapel would cause some discomfort for the new minister, the earnest young and single Reverend Grange. Both of their daughters wanted them all to attend All Saints, which was still presided over by the Reverend Palmer and where they both had fond memories of their earlier singing experiences when they first came to the town. Miss McGregor still sang at St Mary's with a new batch of girls from her school, so it was decided to go to St Mary's by the river bridge with the added advantage that both Peter and Richard were still prominent tenors in the choir there. Emma agreed with this family decision as she secretly felt she should be seen mixing with other tradespeople and Councillors in the town – she was sure Mr. Chapman would have wanted her to. She also hinted to her husband that it could be useful to his business for him to be seen in this popular throng. Bertram had not yet become as sensitive as his wife to local social nuances but he was willing to be converted.

Each Sunday morning therefore, the Moorehouse ladies and Mrs Hyatt sat together near to the front of the principal church in the town on either side of Bertram who was now smiling at his neighbours whilst inwardly knowing that he would not have to lead prayers or give a sermon. An additional advantage of attendance at the principal church was the giving-out of notices informing the attendees of coming services and local events.

On a Sunday morning, a month following the delivery of the new boots to the Brewery, the announcements included the notice of the funeral of Rupert Brandish, to be held on the following Wednesday afternoon. The Brandish family were not regular attendees at St Mary's, since their country home was in the adjacent parish near to the brewery of his wife's family. Hence their recent absence through illness had not been remarked upon. Employees at the Brandish Brewery were used to Rupert's irregular attendance in the office, which they rightly assumed was due to his contact with his wife's family brewery in the adjacent town. Thus, the unexpected funeral of Captain Rupert Brandish was the cause of some speculation. A military event was mentioned with a squad of County Yeomanry to be present as a guard of honour.

Emma walked out of the church close Dr. Smethick-Browne, the medical man who had taken the place of Dr. Redesdale, never seen since his sudden departure from the town years previously, together with his laudanum.

'That was something of a surprise for all of us,' she commented to the doctor. 'I didn't even know he was ill.'

'Ah well,' said the doctor, 'Anthrax is sometimes like that, particularly when it is in the lungs. Rupert thought that he just had a cough with a temperature but then there was a large chest haemorrhage and he died within forty-eight hours. It was probably something he picked up abroad and spores stayed around in his kit. Of course, I have advised that every piece of his clothing be burned along with his boots.'

Emma and Bertram walked home together arm-in-arm, pausing in the middle of the bridge in silence while Bertram smoked another cigar staring thoughtfully at the calm waters.

'You knew that those skins from South Africa were dangerous, didn't you, Bertie. And you let Rupert handle them and smell them.' Emma had an accusative note in her voice. 'You killed him, didn't you?'

'I did not stop him, and he was rather insistent on that particular hide. Anyway, my thoughts were dwelling on ancient cricket matches.'

He took a long, inhaled, draw on his cigar of Zulu herbs whilst watching the slow flow of the water as it passed under the bridge, remaining silent for some minutes.

'Emma, my darling, I am so pleased that we have settled in to this peaceful town and that you and our daughters are living comfortably here. I think we are all going to be very happy with our new lives.' The river current swirled past the bridge's stone pillars, green and silent.

'Did I mention that Reverend Grange asked me if I would look after the Church for him while he visits his mother in Nottingham for a week or two? She is quite ill and apparently London would be happy with this arrangement.'

Emma squeezed her Bertie's hand and put her arm through his as they continued their stroll through the town to their new home.

'What is that tune you are humming, Bertie?' said Emma as they walked together.

'Don't you recognise it? It's *O God Our Help in Ages Past.* I was thinking verse three, or is it four?'

'Is it about the river?' asked Emma.

'Yes, the verse I am thinking about goes like this: "Time, like an ever rolling stream, bears all who breathe away. They fly forgotten as a dream dies at the opening day."' Bertie sighed. 'I was thinking of using these lines as the theme for my next sermon. What do you think?'

'Bertie, I think you may choose anything you like, but please do not mention elephants.'

The couple exchanged a smile as they went through the door of their new cottage.

Lightning Source UK Ltd.
Milton Keynes UK
UKHW011237210119
335933UK00001B/32/P